AN IRISH ROCKSTAR FOR CHRISTMAS

J. SAMAN

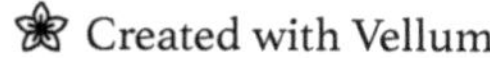
Created with Vellum

1

VIVIAN

Places I hate being most in the world? The airport five days before Christmas. Especially when my flight is delayed an indeterminate amount of time. It's the icing on the shitty couple of months' cake I've been eating like it's my steady diet. All around me children are screaming and fussing. Parents and couples are arguing. People are on their phones, bitching about their delayed or canceled flights.

Everyone is on the last shred of their patience.

If it weren't for the constant stream of cheesy Christmas music and tacky airport decorations, you'd have no clue it was the holiday season as there isn't a drop of cheer in the air.

Doing my best to ignore it all, I take a sip of my wine and continue reading the ARC or advanced reader copy of my best friend's book. This might in fact be her best work yet. She writes action-packed dark 'why choose' romances—my total romance vice—whereas I write steamy rom-coms with an emphasis on athletes—her total vice.

That's how we bonded so quickly when we met at a book signing we both attended in DC two years ago. A friendship I've been more and more grateful for over the past two months when I've been forced to sleep in her guest room. Currently, she's in the Bahamas for the holidays with her boyfriend and I can't help but be a bit jealous of that. I'd rather be sipping margaritas in the sun and having hot, sweaty sex than heading to snowy New England.

That has me slipping out my notebook, flipping to my current page of occupation, and jotting down the words I've written a time or twenty in here. Goal: Be more of a Samantha and less of a Charlotte.

But even as I write the words, recounting the last *Sex and the City* rerun episode I watched where Carrie tells her crew she's moving to Paris to be with her artist boyfriend who we all know isn't the man she's meant to end up with, I know I'll always be stuck in the crux of Charlotte, never brave enough to venture into the land of Samantha. A princess's curse or a lack of a Persephone moment, I'm not sure.

I may love reading all the filth in the world, but I have yet to act out the fantasy of my mind. I'm too cautious. A frown curls the corners of my lips down as I stare at the inked words and then mentally bludgeon myself yet again for staying in my last relationship as long as I did.

Whatever.

I slip my notebook back into my oversized purse. I'm over it. Over him. I think I was before I even found the app on his phone. I'm not even weepy or sad, just annoyed. And... lost. Not from him, but life has me a bit... disjointed. Misplaced. My standard compartmentalization isn't doing its job and I haven't come up with a resolution that doesn't leave me with some lingering form of reconsideration and doubt.

Whatever!

"Excuse me, is this seat taken?"

At the sound of the raspy baritone with an Irish brogue, my head springs up and I lock on the bluest eyes known to man. Artic blue, the color of glaciers and wind but with the warmth of summer smoldering beneath the surface. I blink. Once. Twice. A flush creeps up my cheeks as I take more of him in. Unruly sandy-blond hair buzzed close to his scalp on the sides and long on top to the point where a piece flops playfully against his forehead. Full soft lips, straight nose, and thick, long dark eyelashes that every woman on the planet is jealous of. He has a slight scar going through his right eyebrow and I can't help but wonder how he got it or if it would feel smooth or jagged beneath my finger.

He's wearing a black thermal shirt and dark jeans, but it's his tall stature, along with the way the shirt clings to his built but not bulky muscles that turn my flush into a full-on blush. Because *wow*. That's the word floating like a pretty pink soap bubble through my brain.

He clears his throat, popping that bubble, and I come back to the airport and the noise and misery of it all. Hiding my embarrassment for openly ogling him, I do a quick search around the overly crowded bar I'm sitting in.

"There are no open seats," he supplies for me.

"That's a lie," I tell him, pointing across the bar area to the unoccupied two-person table off in the corner. "There's one over there."

He follows my gaze just as two people scurry over to it, snagging the table.

"Not anymore," he counters, turning back to me with a barely concealed smirk. "Ye see, yer my last hope. Too many delayed flights mean too many people needing a drink to stop them from going postal. Come on. Give me a shot," he continues when I don't automatically relinquish the chair to him. "I won't bother ye too much." He smiles, his hand now on the back of the empty seat directly across from me at my small, high-top two-person table.

"Too much?" I question.

Those sinful blue eyes—crisper than a hundred-dollar bill

in a stripper's G-string—stare into mine with a mischievous sincerity that feels like the ultimate contradiction but somehow works on him. He simply shrugs at me as he takes the seat without waiting on my consent. I don't argue it though. I could listen to his voice and accent all night. In fact, I might have to write an Irish character just so I can have it made into an audiobook, because *damn*.

"Aye. I might bother ye a wee bit. Beautiful redheads shouldn't be sitting alone in airport pubs."

"What makes you think I'm alone?" I retort with a tilt of my head.

That smirk again just as the waitress comes flying over, tripping over two other tables in pursuit of Irish Sex.

"What can I get you?" she rushes out. "Anything to eat. Or drink?"

"Jameson neat, please."

"Double or single?"

"Double." He eyes my red wine. "Make that two doubles, one for the beautiful lady, and keep 'em comin'. Could be a long night." He faces me. "Anything to eat, darlin'?"

My panties are wet. It's not even fair how cheap and easy that happened. I think the waitress agrees with me. I shall name him Irish Sex, which sounds like it could be a drink. I'd ask if they serve that here but given the impish look this guy is all about and how boldly he asked to sit with me, I'm guessing he's a regular at offering up those specific services.

"N-no." I have to swallow and clear my throat. "Just the drinks."

"Same," he tells the waitress. "Thank you."

She sighs but it sounds like a moan, and I can't even blame her for it. I get a "you lucky bitch" glance from her and then she's gone to fetch us our drinks, I presume.

"What makes you think I wanted a whiskey? Or your company for that matter?"

He spins in his seat, shoving up the sleeves of his black shirt and revealing strong, colorfully inked forearms. He intertwines his fingers and sets his hands down on the table like he's about to get down to business. "Ye didn't turn either down. But honestly, it was yer blush that had me sitting. Do ye wanna know a secret?"

"No."

He grins, making some seriously boyishly sexy dimples pop. Somehow he's amused by my less than warm acceptance of his presence.

"Liar," he accuses.

"Only partially."

He belts out a laugh now as I set my e-reader down and slide my half-full wineglass to the waitress when she returns seconds later with the two double whiskeys.

"Are you sure there isn't anything else I can get you? Anything at all?"

"Nah. We're grand," he tells her, and she audibly simpers before skulking away. "Sláinte. It's how you say cheers in Gaelic."

"Sláinte." I lift my class, taking a small sip as he drinks half of his down. "You speak Gaelic?"

"No. Not really. A few words here and there. It's just what my mam always said. Are ye ready for yer secret?"

"Depends." I shift on my stool as I play with the glass in my hands. I'm not a big drinker unless I'm at home with my family, who turns it into a sporting event, but it's been several months.

"On?" he presses.

"I still haven't gotten your name."

A small, bemused chuckle. "Ye don't know it?"

My head bops the other way, my eyebrows narrowing in. "Should I?"

I study him closer, but I'm coming up at a loss. Even as that diabolical smirk turns into a full-on smile, complete with pearly white teeth and twin dimples. He's almost too gorgeous to be real. It's nearly painful. A man who looks like him likely is someone.

"I assumed yer recognizing me was the reason for all yer blushing."

I shake my head, debating between actor and musician. Could be an athlete, but I doubt it since I follow American sports reasonably close given my profession. Possibly be an international soccer player or something, but the waitress seemed to know who he was, so I'm crossing that off my list.

"Are you famous?"

"Suppose it depends on who ye ask and since you don't know who I am, I'm going to say no. I'm Cian O'Connor." He reaches his hand out for me to shake.

"Vivian Scott."

I go to shake his hand but the moment our fingers graze and our palms press a sharp burst of static electricity shocks us. Only it doesn't hurt the way it typically would. This feels warm and tingly like the whiskey in my belly. He feels it too, his oh-so-blue eyes darkening ever so slightly, his grip slipping up to my pulse point, and I inadvertently shiver before I release him. Sliding my hand under the table, I shake it out, trying to clear the tingling that now feels more like a thumping.

"Must be all the static in the air," he muses, almost to himself as the words are low and a bit incredulous.

"Must be," I agree, crossing my legs at the knee and straightening up in my seat. "Alright, Cian. What's this secret you're so anxious to share?" I take another sip of my whiskey, his eyes on my lips as I do.

"It was either I sit with you or the angry bloke muttering to himself over there." He juts his chin over my shoulder, and I turn to look. The man he's referring to is sitting alone at a table like mine and yes, he's fuming as he gripes, staring at his ticket like he wants to ball it up in his fist and throw it away.

I turn back to Cian. "He's not alone. Half the airport is murderous at the moment. All of our flights are either canceled, overbooked, or delayed. Mine is the latter."

"Aye. I was supposed to fly home to Boston, but high winds and icy rain canceled my flight. Best I can do is a flight to Hartford and drive home."

My chest flutters. "That's where I'm flying to." I glance around when I feel that stupid blush start to creep back up my face. "If they don't decide to cancel it, that is."

"Both of us on the same flight? What a fortuitous coincidence. Maybe I'll even get lucky and you'll be sitting beside me."

I flip back over to him accusingly. "You're a bit of a flirt."

"Only with women I'm desperate to impress. Is it working?"

"Not really. I don't tend to be easily impressed by flirts." Especially the cocky, gorgeous ones who are nothing but trouble. They're my book kryptonite and my real-world fear. Then again, playing it safe with the supposed "good guy" never got me anywhere.

He taps his lip in mock contemplation. "Hmmm. What if I offer ye up a desired piece of information? Would that impress ye?"

"Possibly," I retort with a playful grin he instantly matches.

Leaning in against the small table, he encroaches on my personal space, and I catch a hint of his cologne. It's spicy and a bit dangerous. Like fire and leather. "Best I can tell we'll take off in about an hour. That's what the attendant at the desk told me."

Finishing off my drink, I hand it to the waitress just as a new round is delivered. "And you think she told you the truth or was she just trying to get you to smile at her the way every woman in here is?"

He winks at me. "We'll see, won't we? I'm hoping it's the

truth. I'd rather not spend the night in the airport. Unless you agree to do the same with me."

I cover my mouth with my hand, attempting to hide my smile. "That was awful."

He laughs, running a hand through his hair in an almost self-conscious way. "Yer beauty is throwing me off. I'm normally much better at this. You make me nervous, believe it or not." He says that last part almost as if it's an afterthought. A truth, he's remiss to admit.

I peer down at the new drink because even though that sounds like another line, the honesty in his eyes makes my pulse race.

"How about we play a game?"

"A game?" I parrot, eyebrows raised, intrigued.

"A truth for a truth. If we don't answer the other's question, we have to drink."

"If you start asking me my favorite sexual positions or the kinds of kink I'm into, forget drinking, I'll toss my drink in your face."

His hands fly up though there is no hiding his smirk. "Noted. Nothing too sexual. Got it."

I ignore the *too* in that statement. "I should eat something if I'm going to be drinking like this. I was holding out for dinner on the flight, but I think that's ridiculous now. It's already after eight."

"Let me help ye with that." He holds his hand up in the air, signaling our waitress, who once again comes flying over.

"Yes, Mr. O'Connor. Can I get you something?"

My eyebrows hit my hairline. I have to Google him. He's obviously someone.

"What would ye like?" he asks without removing his eyes from mine.

"Grilled cheese and fries, please."

"That sounds good, but now that ye ordered that, I have to

get something different. Em, chicken fingers and sweet potato fries, please," he tells the waitress, still smiling at me.

"Okay," I say the moment she leaves. "You have to tell me. Who are you?"

He shakes his head, sipping at his drink. "No way, darlin'. Ye don't know and I like that about you. Makes you genuine. Yer the first girl I've been able to chat up without knowing if yer talking to me because you like me or ye like what I am."

"Who said I like you?"

He laughs. "Educated guess. Ye haven't gone back to yer book yet nor have ye asked me to leave."

Touché. "How come you won't order the same thing I ordered if you thought it sounded good?"

"Weird tick. I never order the same thing someone else orders and I never order the same thing twice in a restaurant."

Huh. Interesting.

"Now my turn. Tell me what you do for work."

"You won't tell me yours," I counter.

"But yer far more interesting than I am. Come on, Vivie Girl. We've got some time to kill. Play the game with me. I bet I can get ye to reveal all your secrets."

2

VIVIAN

I puff out a breath and take another sip of my whiskey, the alcohol making me bolder and more relaxed than I otherwise would be talking to a complete stranger in an airport bar. A smokin' hot stranger who just gave me a nick-name at that.

"Remember, if ye don't answer my question, then ye have to drink."

"I can't drink like that. If I do, your fan club will be mopping me up off the floor."

"Then I guess ye better answer me."

"I'm an author. I write romance novels."

A smile breaks clear across his face making his dimples pop. He spins his glass around in his hand. "What kind of romance novels?"

"Contemporary rom-coms mostly with sports characters."

"Hmmm. That your type then? Athletes?"

My grilled cheese and his chicken fingers are delivered along with yet another round. At this rate I'll be drunk in no time. At this rate, I'm not sure I care though. Did I not just say I need to be more Samantha and less Charlotte. That I need to stop thinking so much and just *live*.

"I'm not sure I have a type and any type I've had hasn't been the best," I tell him honestly. "I broke up with my boyfriend of two years a couple months ago when I discovered his online dating profile and some of the messages he had been sending to other women. Before that my college boyfriend broke up with me on the night I thought he was going to propose and then he proceeded to screw his way through campus in the last two weeks he was there before he graduated."

"That's rough. I'm sorry." He says it with genuine remorse. "They're fools and that's not a line."

I shrug, taking a bite of my sandwich and wiping my mouth with my napkin. "Thank you. That's another reason I'm heading home besides Christmas. I've been sleeping in my friend's guest room since I broke up with the most recent ex because I'm not sure where I want to go next. I love DC, but I'm thinking it's time for a change."

"Seems like you can live anywhere. Work from anywhere."

"Yes. It's the nice thing about being an author."

"Boston is a fun town. I've lived there since I was in school."

"And before that?"

"Cork County, Ireland. I moved to the States with my mam when I was fourteen or so. My da wasn't the best man and my mam had a friend in Boston."

"Are you going home to visit her?"

He shakes his head, his expression falling. "She died several years back now. Cancer."

"Oh. I'm so sorry." I reach across the table and touch his hand, more of that static charge hitting my skin, and I quickly return to my dinner. "Have you been back to Ireland since you moved to America?"

"No, but I'm funnily enough playing a show in Dublin on New Year's Eve. Not sure if I'll venture out to Cork."

I lift my glass, holding it out toward him. "Musician then? You some kind of rock star since every woman in this bar is drooling over you and our waitress can't help you enough?"

"Fuck," he grouses, running a frustrated hand across his jaw before popping a fry into his mouth. "That just came out, didn't it? Yes. I'm a musician."

I roll my hand in the air, encouraging him to continue. "And you are..."

A grunt.

"Remember, if you don't answer my questions, you have to drink." I blink prettily at him, making him smile.

"Christ, yer a knockout, aren't ye?"

My lips form an *O* shape, but he doesn't miss a beat.

"I'm lead singer fer Reckless Motion." He polishes off his drink even though he answered my question and then digs into his chicken, but I'm still hung up on that.

My hand smacks the table, rattling our drinks.

"What? What's that expression fer?"

"I've heard a few of your songs on the radio. Oh my gosh, how crazy is that? I'm sure everyone does this when they realize who you are, right? Sorry, I ramble when I'm flabbergasted. I'm just shocked because I tend to live mostly in my own tiny bubble. No gossip rags and I don't watch a lot of television. But I've heard of your band. I like you—er—your band that is. Kind of edgy. Not quite rock and not quite alternative."

"That's us."

"Don't worry, I'm still not impressed."

He chuckles as he chews and swallows. "Except I want you impressed, remember? It's liking me because I sing in a band that I don't want."

I think on this for a moment, cradling my drink in my hand as I take him in. "I won't lie and say it's not cool, because it is, and I have no doubt you get laid regularly because of who you are. But"—I hold up my hand when he starts to frown—"you started talking to me and sat down before I knew you were actually famous, and in all honesty, it doesn't make a difference to me either way. I don't think you're hot because you're famous and I don't want to talk to you because of it either."

"See now, all I heard from that amazing speech is that ye think I'm hot and that ye want to talk to me."

"Back to the flirt."

"Darlin', ye make it damn impossible not to flirt. Since we're all so honest tonight and drinking our weight in decent Irish whiskey, I will tell ye that yer the sweetest fucking thing I dare say I've ever seen. I wasn't sitting anywhere else tonight other than here with you."

I blush again—nuclear levels of blushing.

I purse my lips, somehow feeling sour when I have no right to. Maybe it's wondering about all the things my exes were doing behind my back. If they found women like Cian has in a bar, plastered them with alcohol, and sweet-talked them back to a random room for a random night. "Do you use that line on all the groupies?"

He shakes his head, his eyes earnest as they sear into mine. "No. I swear, I've never tried so hard in my life to get a girl to simply smile and talk to me. Certainly never cared if I impressed her or not. Never needed to, which I know sounds bloody awful, but it's still true." A sigh. "Honestly, women come willingly and without effort if I so desire. And until about six weeks ago, I didn't give it much thought. Yer different. I know that. It's why I sat down when I've never been one to make the first move."

"What happened six weeks ago?"

"A story for another time, perhaps. It's frankly not something I'm supposed to talk about. But you? You I'm happy to talk to all night. Flirting or not. As stunning and sexy as I think ye are, we're in an airport killing time. I don't expect anything beyond talking with ye."

I drop my mostly eaten grilled cheese on my plate, wiping my greasy hands on my napkin. "I wish I didn't know who you were."

"Aye. Same here." He gives me a sideways half nod. "So let's pretend I'm just a guy and yer just a girl and this is all so casual and easy."

"All right. I can do that. Favorite animal?" I ask, needing to change the subject to something far safer than the road we're venturing down.

"Dog, though I've never had one. You?"

"Same. We had a dog, Percy, when I was growing up, but he died last year, and my parents haven't replaced him yet."

He finishes his glass, signaling the waitress for another round with the point of his finger. "Ye hangin' alright, darlin'?"

"Not really, but I've decided I'm not a Charlotte tonight. I'm Samantha."

His eyebrows pinch together, and I giggle at how adorable the badass rock star looks when he's confused and amused, and I think I'm rhyming in my head. Drunk. I'm most certainly bordering on drunk territory.

"Are these friends of yers?"

I pop some fries into my mouth, needing grease and carbs to absorb some of the whiskey that's sloshing around in there. "Nope. They're fictional characters in a TV show I'm watching reruns of. Charlotte is the good girl. Always follows the rules. That's me. Forever, that's been me. But Samantha is wild and unbridled and does what she wants without giving a fuck what others think of her."

"Ah, so you've been a good girl, rule follower, and now ye want to be a bit wild and unbridled?"

I throw my hands up, but he points to my drink, indicating I should finish it off and I do because again, fuck it. "I don't know. I'm feeling a bit out of sorts. Maybe it's Christmas or the fact that I'm moving home temporarily without much of a plan for what's next, or the fact that yet another relationship ended on a shitty note."

He leans in, pressing himself against the table to get closer to me. "Want another secret from me?"

I lean in too, mirroring his position and the gesture puts us less than a foot apart. His eyes glimmer, blue ice in the dim lighting of the bar.

"Give it to me."

A grin he battles and loses. "If we weren't headed to different destinations and I weren't leaving in ten days for another four months, I'd spend as much time as I could in bed with ye showing ye just how wild and unbridled ye can be. Ye don't need to be a Samantha or a Charlotte or a whoever. Ye just have to find that side of ye. The one that's anxious for something real."

And once again, my panties are ruined. Soaked. My teeth sink into my bottom lip, and I inadvertently squirm because I bet he's fucking fantastic in bed. He just reeks of "I like to fuck hard and listen as women scream my name in blinding ecstasy." Maybe I'm posturing because it will never ever happen, but yeah, I bet he does all the hot, dirty things I've been missing by dating boring, safe guys who ended up being not so safe.

"You're making me blush again."

"I'm making ye more than that, darlin', I can tell. But since I'm not here to get ye into a quick back-room fuck, how about I ask something safe this time?"

"Please." I fan my face and he laughs. Full-on belly laugh.

"Christ, you'll be the death of me, and I haven't even had a taste. Okay." He straightens up, wiggling his shoulders as if he's getting serious. More drinks—lord help me, my brain is already soft and squishy feeling—and after a sip he licks his lips and nods his head. "Tell me something other people tease you about, but you secretly love about yourself."

That might in fact be the best question anyone has ever asked me.

"I always carry around an extra-large purse because I never leave home without three things. A notebook where I can write down things for myself or thoughts or phrases for a book. My e-reader. And my early edition paperback copy of *Persuasion* by Jane Austen. It's my favorite book and the reason I wanted to become an author."

He leans back in his seat, his gaze all over me as if he's taking me in with new eyes.

"Go on," he says after a moment, his voice thicker and gruffer than it was before, no longer playful. "Tell me more about yer love of *Persuasion*."

"So, it's Jane's last published work and it released on December twentieth, eighteen-seventeen."

"December twentieth? That's today."

"It's also my birthday."

His fingers smack the table, his eyebrows shooting up this hairline. "Today is yer birthday?!" he bellows in shock.

"Twenty-six. Guilty as charged."

"Fuck." His hand flies up in the air. "Can we get one of every dessert ye have on the menu?" he screams over the crowd in the direction of the waitress.

"No!" I cry out. "No, wait. Stop. That's crazy." I practically tumble off my stool.

"Yes. She wants one of every dessert. And another round. Thank you!" He turns back to me, lowering his voice now that half the room is staring at us. "It's yer birthday. We have to celebrate."

My face falls to my hands and I shake my head. "I shouldn't have mentioned it."

"No, ye absolutely should have. Backtracking for a moment, I can't imagine why anyone would make fun of ye for that."

I shrug, my hands falling to my lap. "Well, people think it's odd that I never leave home without it. Not many understand what I do. I write romance, but it's... well... steamy and with that, my exes and my brother believe I only write sex or smut and not love or relationships."

"Hmmm. Well. Em. I disagree with all of them. 'My idea of good company...is the company of clever, well-informed people, who have a great deal of conversation; that is what I call good company.'"

I gasp. And I might die a bit. Because he just quoted it to perfection. "OMG." DEAD!

And possibly in love because let's be honest, how many men who look like Cian O'Connor can quote Jane Austen off the top of their head? None.

"'You are mistaken,' said he gently, 'that is not good company, that is the best.'" I answer from Cornel Wentworth's voice. "How did you know that quote?" I don't think my voice has ever been higher pitched than it is now.

He waves my shocked and awed expression away. And if I'm not mistaken, for the first time tonight, I think I catch a hint of embarrassment beneath his cool, cocky veneer. "It was one of my mam's favorite books too. She was into all the classics and all the romance and used to read them to me when I was a lad. Made me read her *Persuasion* and *Wuthering Heights* twice each when she was sick, which is why I know the quote so well."

Yep. Totally in love with this stranger.

"All right, you managed it. I'm officially impressed. Very impressed. I'm also impressed by how much you can drink." Two more glasses are placed in front of us, and I realize I haven't even finished my last one whereas he has. I've lost count how many this makes. "Damn. I've had... two, three of these, and I'm definitely feeling it."

He runs a hand through his blondish hair, brushing some of those longer strands on top from his face and giving me a sinful view of the ink on the underside of his forearm. "Irish blood. It's a cliché, but a useful one. If it helps, I don't normally drink like this. It's been a long bloody day in the airport with a long bloody night ahead of me."

"Are you heading home for Christmas?"

"Something like that. Our third album comes out in January, which is when we start our tour in Europe. I haven't been home in over six months. My bandmates all went home to their families and well, I guess I'll have a week and a half of quiet before I have to get back to it."

"Does that mean you're spending Christmas alone?"

He smiles but it doesn't touch his eyes. He opens his mouth to answer when our flight is announced over the loudspeaker, informing us it's going to be boarding in a few minutes. I hop out of my seat a bit too fast before my brain can catch up. Feeling momentarily dizzy, all the alcohol hitting me at once, I latch on to the table to steady myself.

"Whoa, are ye okay?" Cian too leaps out of his chair, grasping onto my hips to help steady me. His touch is about all I can feel right now, the rest of me is drunkenly numb. "I think maybe I got ye one too many whiskeys. Do ye need help?"

"No. I'm fine. Thank you." I force myself to glance up. And wow, he truly is something else. I clear my throat and snatch my purse—before I grab his face and maul him right here—and start to pull out some money, anxious to get on the plane and get home.

"It's on me," he tells me, placing his hand over mine to stop my movements. I want to object, but he's insistent. "It's yer birthday, Vivian, plus I monopolized your reading time and barged in on yer table. You've graciously put up with me trying to flirt and impress you. Please, I'd like to pay."

"Okay. Thank you." I hesitate, feeling strange leaving him here when we're about to get on the same flight.

"I'm sorry we didn't get to eat yer desserts."

"Me too."

"I'll see ye on board, maybe," he murmurs as if reading my mind.

"Hope so." And I mean it. I only just met him, and I realize I'll likely never see him again, but oddly the thought of that makes me sad. I like talking to him. I like the way he looks at me. The way he's made me feel in just the hour or so we've been sitting here together.

Bouncing up on the balls of my feet, I reach up and place a kiss on his cheek.

He touches where my lips just were, a bemused grin on his lips. "What was that fer?"

"For dinner. For Christmas. For wanting to impress me. For quoting my favorite book to me. I'll see you on the plane."

I scoot off, wheeling my carry-on behind me, heading for the ladies' room.

A sexy Irish rock star just bought me whiskey and a grilled cheese. And I think I might like him. Drunk flutters and all.

3

CIAN

Vivian turns and walks away, and I feel something tug in my stomach. It's as if my body naturally wants to follow hers. It quirks an odd sort of frown to my lips because I'm positive I've never felt anything like it before and I can't quite make sense of it. It's just desire, I wager. That's all this must be. I haven't met a woman I cared enough to talk to or who wasn't only talking to me because of my name in a very long time.

But more than that, I haven't met anyone I want to spend more time with in years.

I haven't kissed her or touched her, and, in all likelihood, I never will. Even knowing that, I still want more time with her.

Look back, darlin'. Let me know it's not just me feeling this.

She turns as if she heard the plea from my lips and when she catches me watching her, a soul-stealing smile lights up her face as does that alluring blush I've been treated to a few times. She offers me a timid wave and then scurries off with quick steps toward the toilets.

It'll never happen, I tell myself. Best to let it go now.

Clearing my thoughts of her, I text my best friend and lead

guitarist, making sure he got on his plane to Chicago okay. He was delayed for a while too. I've been in this airport for the better part of five hours now and my lovely redhead was the first thing to make me laugh or smile in... weeks. It's been weeks at least if I'm being honest with myself.

The road takes its toll, but this break... going home to an empty flat in a city where I no longer know anyone or have any family...

I've been dreading Christmas as I've dreaded it every year since Mam passed.

But Vivian somehow made me forget everything for that hour. A woman who is so stunningly beautiful my breath caught in my chest when I saw her. I was sideswiped. Thunderstruck. And I knew I wasn't going anywhere until I spoke to her.

She's a sonnet. An epic ballad. An anthem. And I want her.

Pulling out my notebook, I quickly jot that down before tucking it back in my pocket. She said people made fun of her for carrying around a notebook, but clearly that's something she and I have in common. Both authors, artists, though her words end up in books and mine in songs.

Me: Are you on the plane?

Everett: Yes. Not too late to change your mind. There's an open seat beside me.

Me: Go be with your family and enjoy your Christmas. I'll see you in Dublin.

Everette: The invitation is a standing one. Think about it.

I did think about it and last year I was with his family over the holidays. But even though they're gracious, wonderful people, they already have enough of their own family to deal with without me being thrown into that. I'll go home and be alone in my misery. It's how good songs are written anyway. I'll drink whiskey and eat bad takeout and write the words I need to write and maybe even venture out and fuck a woman or two. It'll be fine.

That's what I've been telling myself and it's getting to the point where I've almost convinced myself I'll even enjoy the solitude and won't be depressed as fuck.

Shaking off the thoughts, I crack on and meander my way toward my gate, stopping briefly to grab some sweets before the flight and then the two-hour drive after in shite weather. By the time I make it to the gate, first class has already boarded and there are lines of people waiting for their turn. I glance about, but I don't see my redhead. Maybe she's late.

A few people start to murmur, glancing in my direction and I scoot myself in line, scan my ticket, and then make my way down the walkway toward the plane. Our record label and producer, Lyric Rose discovered us playing in a bar in LA. She signed us that night and within three months, our first album hit top ten on the charts, skyrocketing us from four guys who liked to play in bars and for friends into the limelight, complete with social media growing by the millions.

Our second album was an even bigger success, and thus that's what we've become as a result.

I'm not used to being recognized. I'm not sure I ever will be.

I still think of myself as a poor kid from Cork with a da who liked to smack his wife around and a mam who worked two jobs to support her son. The one main regret I have is that I wasn't able to provide a better life for my mam before she died. Her life was nothing but pain and sacrifice and it still tears me up I couldn't have done more for her.

Hunching my shoulders forward, cold air seeps through my shirt as I keep my head down, stepping onto the plane—right foot first for luck always. The moment I turn the corner onto the plane, eyes the color of summer grass meet mine from the second-row window in first class. My heart skips a beat as it did when I first saw her.

No way in hell I'm not sitting beside her on this flight.

Tossing her a wink, I immediately go up to her seatmate.

"Excuse me, miss," I say to the adorable elderly woman who isn't bigger than a pint glass. "I'm so sorry to bother ye, but I'm sitting right here in row four on the aisle. Would you mind switching seats with me, so I can sit next to my girlfriend?"

Vivian coughs in surprise, her face once again turning the same lovely shade as her hair. I half expect her to call me out on my brazen move, but she sits there quietly. Even smiling softly as the elderly woman turns to her.

"Sure. Of course." The woman starts to rise out of her seat, and I offer her my hand.

"May I help you?"

"A gentleman," the woman replies with a flutter of her own.

"My mam always told me that there is nothing wrong with treating a woman as a woman as long as ye respect her as an equal."

She places her small, cold hand in mine, and I help her to stand. "He's a keeper, this one," she says to Vivian who is still too stunned to say much.

Vivian murmurs out a small, "Thank you," and then I'm helping the woman into her new seat.

"Thank you. I greatly appreciate it. I hate being separated from her, even on this short flight." I give the woman my most charming grin and then quickly take my seat beside Vivian as I've started to cause a small backup of people getting on the plane. "Well then," I say as I buckle my seat belt and settle in. "This is a grand coincidence."

"Boyfriend?" she questions with a raised eyebrow.

I shrug. "Easy as anything to say. I was worried I'd already missed ye."

"Same," she tells me, and a foreign sensation hits my chest. A lightness maybe. "I think you also got me a little drunk."

Shifting in my seat, I find a strand of her silky hair that's hanging down around her arm and drag it between my fingers. I can't help but touch her. I'm nearly giddy that I get more time with her and I'm having trouble reining it in. "Sorry about that. Were ye sick?"

"No. Just a bit dizzy for a little."

"Shite." I turn toward the flight attendant. "Can we get a water, please?"

"Of course, sir."

She goes to get Vivian a water. First class has its perks.

I turn back to Vivian, making sure her eyes are clear enough. "Will ye forgive me for getting ye so bladdered?"

"Bladdered?"

"Trashed, I think is how you'd say it."

"Yes," she whispers, her eyes dark and heavy, our bodies close despite the barrier between our seats. "But only because I Googled you. You've got a bad boy reputation and a heart of gold, it seems."

I snicker at the earnest way she says that. "Ye can't believe everything ye read on social media. I could be the devil incarnate."

"You were raised in foster care after you lost your mom to cancer."

I look toward the aisle, at the people filing in, searching for their seats. I take a second to suppress the familiar jolt of pain I always feel when I think about my mam and what happened after she died. "Yes."

"That must have been hard."

I nod, still unable to meet her eyes. "Aye. It was."

"Wanna know a secret?" she asks, throwing my words from earlier back at me.

Now I can't help but stare into her pretty eyes again. "I wanna know everything about you." And those words, my words, they come out different than hers. They come out a touch desperate. A slight bit needy. Maybe it's that she's reminded me of what I endured after losing my mam. Maybe it's all the lost hours in the airport or the vat of whiskey we drank. Maybe it's fucking Christmas, a holiday I hate most of all.

But I suddenly wish I was her boyfriend and had infinite time with her. That this was a transatlantic flight. I wish we had hours in the air together instead of just one and some change. The way she looks at me stirs my blood.

"I blushed because I thought you were gorgeous. Not because I knew who you were. And knowing who you are now, well, I still think you're gorgeous, but I think I liked you more before I knew you were famous. If that makes sense."

I laugh under my breath. "Just how drunk are ye, Vivie Girl?"

"Drunk enough to tell you the truth."

I lean in and kiss the tip of her nose. I hardly know this woman, but I feel close to her in a way I haven't earned. In a way I'm not sure I deserve. "I liked you instantly. Before I ever spoke to you. I liked yer hair and the fact that yer smiling face was buried in your e-reader, oblivious to the mayhem and frustration of the people around ye. But when ye looked up and quickly glanced about, I knew there was nowhere else I was going than beside you."

The flight attendant delivers us both some waters and Vivian takes a sip, setting it down on the flat surface between our seats. "Tell me your favorite thing about playing music."

"Are we still playing our game then?" I tease. "Because I don't think ye can handle any more whiskey."

"No, I just want to know more about you."

The flight attendants go through their safety speeches, the plane starting to pull back from the gate, but it's as if it's just the two of us in our own little world.

"Music was all I had for myself for a while. My mam had saved up every penny she could and bought me a guitar when I was thirteen. Three years later, she was gone, but I held on to that guitar like it was my lifeline. It was my constant. My only friend sometimes. So I played and I sang and I wrote songs. I love how easy it is fer me to get lost in music. How it fills not only my soul but the souls of others. If I can write a song that speaks and heals someone else the way music speaks and heals me, well, what could be better than that?"

Curling herself up on her seat, her head falls to my shoulder.

"I think you're pretty amazing. I listened to a few more of your songs before I got on the plane. "Were you discovered in Boston? Is that how it happened for you?"

"No. When I graduated high school, I moved out to LA and met my current bandmates at the bar we were all working in. We started playing some local bars and a few clubs and then we caught the eye of Lyric Rose who owns Turn Records. She signed us and then Eden Dawson produced our album and it just hit. It was savage. I never expected anything like this to happen. Don't know what to do with it half the time."

"Can't be too bad having women fall all over you and getting to travel the world," she murmurs, her voice thick and sleepy.

Turning my face, my nose dives into her hair and I inhale her sweet fragrance. It's warm and heady, like roses and sunshine. "I'm mostly a loaner so it's not all as glamorous as it sounds. And well, I think right now, there's only one woman I'd like to have fall all over me."

She doesn't reply and I peek down to find her eyes closed and her breathing even. Chuckling to myself, I carefully adjust our position so my arm is around her and she's tucked tighter into me. It also gives me a better vantage of her face and for the longest time as we take off and lift into the air, I watch her. Wondering how we even got here. I only met her tonight and now she's sleeping on me. Sweet and peaceful and so fucking gorgeous my head spins.

Can you like someone like this so soon?

I kiss her forehead, allowing my lips to linger on her skin likely longer than I should. The thought of simply walking away from her when we get to Hartford sits like sour milk in my gut. She'll be with her family, and I'll be home alone and thinking about her. Wondering what could have been if circumstances were different. If I hadn't met her in an airport. If I had met her...

It doesn't matter, and I shouldn't be thinking like this.

On New Year's Eve, we'll be in Ireland and then on the road for the next four months touring through Europe and parts of Asia. Then it's back to LA and into the studio. It's a never-ending cycle. One that doesn't lend itself well to steady women or real lives. That's what makes the groupies so perfect and easy.

No, this is only going to be a stolen moment in time. Something I'll remember and keep with me. The night I met the most incredible girl and found myself wishing that everything could be different. Even if it never will be.

4

CIAN

Vivian wakes with a jolt when the plane touches down on the runway, her body jerking upright. Disoriented, she searches around, and finally her gaze snags on mine. "Sleep well," I tease, my expression nothing if not amused and playful.

"Oh god," she murmurs, clapping her hand over her mouth. "Did I fall asleep on you?"

I chuckle, reaching over and brushing some wild strands of her hair back from her face. I can't seem to stop touching her, especially her hair that I might be a bit obsessed with. It looks like blood flowing through my fingers but feels like the finest silk.

"Ye did, but don't worry, you were adorable and it's my fault anyway for getting ye as drunk as I did."

"True. We'll blame you for that. I'm not used to drinking whiskey by the barrel. At least I didn't drool on you." She laughs, scrunching her nose. "You were an excellent pillow."

"I'm happy to hear it. And you're welcome to sleep on me any time. But straight truth, I also may have kissed yer forehead and smelled yer hair."

"Flirt," she accuses, but there is no heat in her tone or expression. Yawning, she turns toward the window, sliding up the shade and peering out. "Oh wow, it's really snowing."

"Aye. It seems what's wind and icy rain in Boston is snow here. The weather app on my phone says yer to get a foot or so tonight."

"And you have to drive home in this? It's already so late." She turns back to me in time to catch my shrugging like it's not that big of a deal—I'm not so excited about it, but what am I to do or say—and then silence falls between us. An edgy silence. The sort of silence that acknowledges our time together is just about up and neither of us wants it to be.

If she were any other woman, I'd already be in bed with her.

I could stay at the airport tonight. Ask her to stay with me though I know she needs to get home to her family and would say no—she's not a one-night girl. I could find a hotel room and sleep and then drive home in the morning, but I'm so bloody tired of hotel rooms. At this point, after the day I've had, if I can't be with Vivian, I just want to get home.

The plane comes into the gate and the loud ding sounds overhead, everyone shuffling and getting out of their seats, anxious to get to baggage claim and then get out of the airport. I stand, reaching my hand out for hers and helping her to do the same. Only the moment her skin touches mine and I get a flash of that charge between us, I don't let it go.

I can't.

I need to be close to this woman for as long as I can. It's not even rational. I know it's not. But somehow in the few hours I've spent talking with her and touching her and staring at her, I like her. And I can't even tell you the last time I liked a woman. There is something about her and I don't want that to be over. Not yet.

I continue to hold it, even as we exit the plane and walk

through the mostly deserted terminal. Bradley airport is small, and it doesn't take us long to get to the escalator that leads us down to baggage claim and over to our carousel.

"How are ye getting home?" I ask as the buzzer cries loudly through the air, flashing a red light, and the carousel starts to move.

"I was going to call my dad initially, but it's so late I don't want to wake him. Or have him drive in this weather. I think I'll just Uber home or take a cab."

I'm shaking my head before she's even done speaking. "I'll drive ye."

"No. That's crazy. It's in the complete opposite direction from where you need to go."

"It's late, Vivian. I don't feel right about ye getting into a cab or a strange car. I'm already going to be on the road."

"But—"

I step into her, cutting her off, my fingers playing with hers. They're small and thin and delicate, just like her. She's petite, sure, despite having some generous curves in all the right places that tempt every ounce of the devil in me, but her facial features are so delicate there is something goddess-like about her. Any touch I'm allowed is a gift.

"Let me drive ye home, okay? Ye know me. Ye looked me up, so ye know who I am and that you'll be safe with me. If I only get another hour with ye, I'd like to have it."

She swallows thickly, her green eyes flickering back and forth between mine. She's shy and a bit nervous, but there is a boldness to her, something I saw almost instantly back in the bar earlier that shines through.

"Okay," she finally says. "Thank you. I'd appreciate a ride home if it's not too much trouble."

"The only trouble I'm gonna have is saying goodbye."

With that truth floating between us, I release her hand and both of us wait at the carousel for our bags to come off. I grab mine and my baby, otherwise known as my guitar, and then hers comes almost immediately after it, and then we're out in the cold, under the overhang with snow falling in between the breaks of concrete above us.

Vivian shivers, and I open the outer zipper pocket of my suitcase and drape my coat over her shoulders. "Where's your coat, darlin'?"

"In my suitcase." She laughs the words. "I didn't think much about it when I packed everything up."

"Mr. O'Connor," a man cries my name, jogging over to us. "Here are your keys, sir. The car is all set for you, and Mr. Craigsworth has ensured it's yours until the thirtieth. Is there anything else I can get you?"

I take the keys from the man's hand and that's when I notice the sleek black Range Rover parked along the curb and running.

"No. This is fantastic. Thank you so very much." I shake the man's hand, slipping him some money.

"Thank you, sir."

Before I can respond with, I hate being called sir, the man is grabbing my suitcase by the handle along with Vivian's, walking them over to the car. He takes both of our bags and sets them in the trunk as I help Vivian into the warm passenger side. Shutting the door behind her, I thank the man again and then climb into the driver's side, turning on Vivian's seat warmer and pointing the vents in her direction.

"Must be good to be you. I've never seen anyone deliver a car like this at the airport in the middle of the night."

"Has its perks sometimes," I admit.

She continues to shiver, tucking into my coat and I already know I'm going to be a fool and bury my nose in the fabric of it once she's handed it back to me and all this is over between us. I ask for the address of her parents' home and once I put it into my phone's navigation system that plays on the screen of the car, we set off into the snow. It's slick and quiet, the hour late and the night dark despite the small white flakes falling in fast quantities from the sky.

We listen to music, and I ask her about her writing. The sort of stories she's done and what her career is like. She's a big deal, though she tries to play it down. I Googled her too while she was asleep on me and the number of books she's written, along with the accolades they've received, is evident. Impressive. She tells me about her family. About her brother and his wife and her wee nieces. About her parents who are great and have always been supportive of her and her career.

We laugh and she teases me about how I don't play any of my own songs—never have and never will. And when I tell her how I don't have any of my own on my phone, she goes all holy joe at that and scrolls through the songs on my phone, haughty like and thinking she'll prove me wrong only to discover I'm telling the truth.

I drive slowly, carefully, for her and to keep this ride going a bit longer, and after more than half an hour, we pull into the driveway of her parents' house. It's a big, nice-looking house. Very New England and on a sweet little suburban street, lined with similarly sized houses. The car in park, I turn to her at the same moment she turns to me.

Words stick in my throat and because of that, she beats me to it with, "I think you should spend the night." She blurts it out hastily, but the moment the words hit the air between us, she squares her shoulders, and her eyes hold on to mine.

"What? Spend the night here at your parents'?"

"Yes. Look at it out here." She pans her hands toward the windows that are already streaked with icy snow. "It's awful out, and it's close to midnight now. It's late and dangerous. You have to stay. You took all this extra time to drive me home."

I blink at her, a bit surprised, I think, and then glance

toward her house trimmed in glowing gold Christmas lights. I turn back to her. "Won't yer parents mind?"

An adamant headshake. "No. Not at all. I'll put you on the pullout in my dad's office since he'd never let you sleep in my room even with the bunk beds and likely Peter and Hazel and the girls are in the other two rooms," she rambles on, almost nervously as if I was going to suggest sleeping in her bed. I'd love nothing more than that, but it'd be wrong in her parents' house. I'm about to argue further when she reaches over and takes my hand. "Please stay. You can't drive two hours in this. It's not safe and it's already so late."

And because right now I'd do just about anything she asked of me, I say, "Okay. I'll stay the night. Thank you."

With a relieved smile, she gives my hand a squeeze before hopping out of the car. We fly around to the trunk, grabbing our bags and my guitar, and then leg it up the slippery steps, anxious to get inside and out of the freezing cold and snow.

Before she can unlock the door, it swings open with a man I presume to be her dad on the other side, looking rumpled and sleepy. "You were supposed to call," he tells her, grabbing her and dragging her in for a hug.

"I texted before I took off saying I'd get another ride. I wasn't going to let you come out in this."

"Hi baby. I'm glad you're home. I missed you. Happy birthday."

"Hi Daddy." She pulls back, laughing at the hint of emotion in her eyes. "Dad, I want to introduce you to someone. This is Cian O'Connor. He's a friend of mine and he drove me home tonight. With the snow and the late hour, I told him he could sleep on the couch in your office."

"It's nice to meet you, sir."

Her dad eyes me up and down, making a face and yep, fathers never liked me much. Tattoos and a bad boy air always raise their hackles when it comes to me with their daughters.

It's like no matter how much money I make, I'll always be the poor Irish boy who spent his teenage years bouncing from one foster home to the next.

Stepping back, he allows us to come in before he shuts and locks the door behind us. We stand in a foyer close to the bottom of the stairs. It smells like freshly baked cookies and cinnamon, the room bathed in the soft glow of the Christmas lights twined around two pillars that lead into a formal parlor.

"It's nice to meet you too, Cian." Her dad shakes my hand, a firm grip I return because this is what men do to size each other up and show their respect, strength, and purpose. "You're welcome to stay, son, but unfortunately you can't sleep on the couch in my office," he whispers, likely so he doesn't wake anyone up.

Vivian's brows pinch. "Why not?"

"Because someone is already sleeping on it."

"Who?"

"Hunter."

"Hunter?" Vivian squawks sharply. "As in Hunter Brooks? Why the hell is Hunter here?" Her voice rises on the last part and her father makes a gesture with his hands for her to keep her voice down.

He gives her a sympathetic look. "He's staying through Christmas. Your brother invited him."

Her hands fly about as she grows more agitated. "And why isn't he with his family? He's never here for Christmas. Never."

"They're in Europe."

Her cheeks grow hotter by the second. "So what? He should be with them. Not here. Dad, this is so messed up."

"I wasn't exactly consulted on it," her father says in a quiet tone. "He spoke with your mother and Peter, and both of them failed to tell me about it."

"Because they knew how I'd feel about it and that you'd take my side." Vivian paces a small circle while I watch on, at a complete loss other than she clearly doesn't like this Hunter bloke.

"I'm sorry, who is Hunter Brooks?" I cut in, because if I can't sleep here then I need to go, but I also don't want to leave and have her here with this guy she obviously doesn't want to be near.

"Her brother's best friend and her ex-boyfriend," comes a voice from behind me, and I whip around to take in the tall man with dark, sleep-tousled hair and equally dark eyes wearing a white T-shirt and red flannel pants.

"The one ye recently broke up with?" I ask Vivian, my gaze slingshotting from Hunter back to her.

"No. The one before that one. My college boyfriend."

I think about what she said to me tonight at the bar. She mentioned a college boyfriend who she thought was going to propose, only he broke up with her to screw around with women immediately after. That must be this arsehole. Rich-looking prick with his expensive haircut and preppy boy good looks, I've gone up against his type my whole life. I also have a few inches of height on him and about ten pounds of muscle. Not to mention I grew up with an arsehole father in Ireland and then in foster care.

I could kill him with my bare hands, but he's not small, and he wants me to know it as he straightens up and gives me what I presume to be his tough-guy glare. I offer up a cocky smirk in return, even if my insides are swaying.

Fuck.

Vivian shifts her stance, visibly frowning, not happy at all to see him. "What are you doing here?"

"I was invited to spend Christmas with your family. I haven't spent any length of time with Peter in a while, and well, I knew you'd be here."

Hunter crosses the room and wraps her up in a hug, kissing her cheek, and I see red. A haze that coats me with its own distinct flavor and texture. A haze of anger and jealousy and resentment I've breathed before, only this one's more potent somehow. Different in that it's over a woman. A red I have zero right to and frankly don't fully understand all that well, but yeah, I want to rip the geebag apart for touching her.

"It's good to see you, Viv. It's been too long. You look beautiful. Your hair is longer now."

Her arms rest at her sides and when he lingers longer than I like, instinctively I reach out, practically prying her away from him until she's standing beside me. My hands clasp her waist, steadying her, and she glances up at me with an unreadable expression.

"And who's this?" Hunter's eyes narrow in on my hands on Vivian before giving me a haughty glare that makes my fist clench.

"This is Cian O'Connor—"

"Her boyfriend," I cut her off, gripping her waist tighter when she understandably stiffens against me. Because... the fuck did I just do? I said it earlier tonight on the plane, but that was a joke. This is a territory I've just staked, and it has my heart thrashing wildly in my chest. The words tumbled out, indignant and feral and possessive, and now they're there and I can't take them back. I wanted to wipe the smug grin from his face with one of my own, and I did manage that, but now...

"Her what?" comes from both her father and Hunter. She moves to swivel in my arms, but my grip won't allow it. Instead, I shift her until she's tucked into my side. I can feel her heavy, uneven breathing, her body a wall of confusion and unease, and understand she's likely furious with me.

Pretending to be her boyfriend to her father and ex wasn't exactly part of the plan for tonight.

"Her boyfriend," I repeat because she hasn't exactly disagreed with me, and I've already started this party. "Vivie

Girl and I have been together for... what is it? Six weeks or so now?"

Slowly her head tilts up, her green eyes wide and unsure, and I wonder if I messed up the timing. She did recently break up with someone, but she had said a couple months ago. Her lips part as she studies me, and I do my best to say go with it with my eyes, but I'm not sure that's what she wants. She'd be well within her right to kick me in the bollocks.

With her silence, my heart thrashes harder as my palms start to sweat. I have no idea what to say and I don't think she does either. I can see the warring question on her face: Do I lie and tell my father and Hunter that Cian is my boyfriend?

"Vivian?" Hunter presses when she doesn't back up my story. Shite. They're going to kick my arse in a minute and toss me out back into the snow.

"Um. Yes." She clears her throat as something close to a twisted smile curls slightly at the corner of her lips. "I think it's been about that long."

A breath I didn't realize I was holding flees my lungs and I press her tighter against me, feeling triumphant somehow though I have no idea what I'm doing or how we'll pull this off or even what it means for me leaving tomorrow.

"But you broke up with that other guy only two months ago," Hunter maintains, his arms folding over his chest as he stares skeptically at us.

"I met Cian in a bar a couple weeks later," she counters. "He came up to me and asked if he could sit with me. We started casually dating and then progressively got more serious."

"You're joking," Hunter throws out, examining me closer now, glaring at the tattoos peeking out from beneath the sleeves of my sweater and rough jeans. "This guy isn't your type at all. He's poor Irish trash."

I bristle at that if only because it's the story of my life. "I wouldn't be so sure of that, mate. Besides, her old type seems to be useless scuts who take her for granted. That's certainly not me. She's my perfect mix of Samantha and Anne Elliott."

Vivian sputters out some kind of unintelligible sound, but her eyes instantly glass over as she stares up at me. "You think so?"

"Absolutely, darlin'. No doubt about it." Even if I'm not quite sure who Samantha actually is. I kiss the tip of her nose. "Breathe, Vivie," I murmur, and she exhales immediately.

"Bullshit. What does that even mean? Who are Samantha and Anne Elliott?" Hunter grits his teeth, his jaw clenching, but I continue to stare straight into his eyes, refusing to back down.

"You not knowing tells me ye don't know my Vivian as well as ye play."

"You better watch—"

Hunter advances a small step when Vivian's father steps between us, holding out his hand to Hunter, stopping him. "I'm going to bed," her father declares, cutting the tension. "I think it's best if all of you do the same. Cian, since Hunter is occupying my study, you can sleep in Vivian's room, but only on the bottom bunk. Vivian, you're on the top, am I understood?"

Vivian's eyes go round and I'm assuming she's not used to her dad allowing boys up in her room for the night. Something about the fact that he's letting me, a man he just met and now thinks is dating his daughter, fills my chest with warm gratitude and tugs a smile to my lips.

I reach my hand out to shake his again. "Thank you, sir. Bottom bunk. Promise."

He shakes my hand with a nod that tells me he's trusting me, which is certainly more than I was ever expecting. "Vivian, you might want to keep Cian away from your mother for both our sakes. A hundred bucks says she throws herself all over him when she realizes who you brought home with you. She's a huge fan of his, if you didn't already know. She and Hazel were watching and singing along to a YouTube video of his band just tonight."

And with that declaration that has me chuckling under my breath, he ambles up the steps leaving the three of us alone in the foyer.

5

VIVIAN

I have absolutely no clue what just happened. One minute I was begging Cian to spend the night and then the next Hunter is here like the ghost of Christmas past and now somehow Cian is my... fake boyfriend? And my mother and sister-in-law are fans of his? And Hunter is glaring. Hard.

Like a fire-breathing dragon, all red faced and brown eyed, angry as if Cian stole the princess from the castle he was keeping her locked up in. Only, Hunter has no right to any ounce of jealousy or anger. None. Zero. Zip. Nada.

"Band?" Hunter snarls out. "You're what... some kind of rock star?" The mocking disdain in his voice cracks like a whip.

"Something like that, yeah," Cian says, cool as ever.

Hunter turns his malice onto me. "Vivian, since when do you give a shit about or even notice rock stars? You break up with your boyfriend and turn into some kind of groupie?"

I open my mouth to verbally eviscerate him when Cian says, "Actually, Vivian had no clue who I was when we first met. And she's the furthest thing from a groupie there is." Cian takes a step in front of me, encroaching on Hunter's space enough to make his physical presence more pronounced. "And let me warn ye now, mate. If ye ever speak down to Vivian again, I will show you just how well poor Irish trash brawls."

Hunter sputters out a pathetic attempt at a spoiled, rich-boy scoff.

Cian turns around, giving Hunter his back, showing him just how unafraid he is of him. "Vivie, if yer keen, I'm shattered and since ye slept a bit on the plane, I'm sure ye are too. How about we go on up and leave Hunter to himself?"

"Good idea." I twist around Cian to catch Hunter's face. He's staring at me as if he doesn't know what to do or think or say, but it all has a strong undercurrent of helpless agitation. In all the years he and I dated, he was never allowed to sleep in my bedroom. My father never liked him. He tolerates him as Peter's best friend, but never liked the two of us as a couple. Now the first night Dad meets Cian, and he's fine with him sleeping in my room?

I don't get it, but I'm not about to question it either.

I should have listened to my dad. Hunter was a chronic gaslighter, and I was too young and too besotted and too much of a good girl to question anything other than to hate his flagrant disapproval of everything I was. The best thing about a breakup is that it forces you to remove the rose-colored glasses you were wearing and see your relationship for what it truly was.

Without a glance toward Hunter, we head for the stairs.

"Vivian. Listen, I'm sorry, okay? I just didn't expect you to be with someone else already, and certainly not someone like him," Hunter says, stopping my motions if only for a second. His voice is softer now, his eyes beseeching. "I was hoping we could talk?"

"Maybe tomorrow. It's late, and as Cian said, I'm tired."

Cian grabs one of my bags and I snag another and then I'm leading us upstairs, treading quietly so I don't wake up the rest of the sleeping house. Opening the door to my room, for a moment I get a burst of girlish embarrassment. It's the same as it was when I was in high school. Lavender walls and bookshelves filled with books and gymnastics trophies.

Cian steps in behind me, and I shut the door, locking it though I'm positive my father won't like that so much. Cian's breathing hard, taking in my room as well as the bunk beds in the corner before spinning around to face me.

"I'm so sorry," he starts. "I don't know why I did that. He was staring at me all smug like, which bothered me more than it should have. It was like high school all over again and I stupidly reacted. But ye seemed so upset about him being here and then when ye told me who he was, I remembered what ye had said in the airport, and I… I don't know. I wanted to make it easier on ye but also, I…"

He trails off, his electric-blue eyes wild. Frantic.

"Also, you what?"

He blinks before his gaze drops to the pale hardwood floors and thick gray area rug. He lets out a heavy sigh. "Also, I was jealous. I didn't like that he was here for you. That he was going to get more time with you when I wasn't. That he could have a shot when I couldn't."

Butterflies slam into me, making a stupid blush creep up my face. I don't know if it's because I'm in my parents' house in my old bedroom or what, but suddenly I feel like a girl who's been crushing on the bad boy at school, the one every girl wants, and he finally noticed me. Me! The lowly book nerd. It's heady and weird and I like how it feels far too much considering the odd situation we now find ourselves in.

I could tell the truth. Come out about it to everyone. But… I don't want to.

I want Cian to be my fake boyfriend.

I want an excuse to look at him and touch him. Even if it's short lived. It's stupid and reckless and likely to blow up in my face, but what the hell. It's something straight from a romance novel and I'm here for it. Even knowing there is no option for making it real or falling in love.

He's leaving to tour Europe and my situation is too unsettled.

Plus, let's be real here, he's a freaking rock star. Chances that he wants an actual girlfriend latching on to him are zilch. He might want sex and he might be jealous in a territorial male sort of way, but I have no illusions about what's real here and what isn't.

So, even though this has romance book glory written all over it, I already know we won't end in a HEA or even an HFN. That understanding will need to chill in my brain on a perpetual repeat, because the way Cian stood up for me to Hunter? That wasn't even part of his role as boyfriend. That was the real deal. I could feel the burn of it flaming off Cian's skin.

I step into him a bit and run my fingers up through his hair because I feel like I can. His head comes up along with my touch, his eyes flickering back and forth between mine with uncertainty.

"This is insane to do with a stranger."

"Vivian, I don't know what it is about ye, but ye don't feel like a stranger to me. I'm not sure ye ever did."

The intensity in his eyes, even the darkness pulls at places I'd just assume lock down when it comes to a man like Cian. Rock star. Famous. Has women all over him. I've had enough of womanizing assholes.

But Cian doesn't feel like that and I'm not even sure why.

A yearning, a bubbling wish I have no business making hits my brain hard, practically shooting itself up into the sky and latching on to the first star it comes across. It's a wanting. A desire for more of him. A hope he doesn't flee at first dawn.

"I love scrambled eggs and hate French toast. My favorite food is grilled cheese, as you might have already learned tonight. I'm homeless after breaking up with my ex. My family knows this, and I already told you about that earlier. Hell, at this point, I think I told you all there is to know about me."

He smirks. "Aye. I also learned yer an easy drunk."

"I'm what many would call quirky."

"I like that about ye. I think I have a touch of that myself."

"What's your favorite book?"

"*The Importance of Being Earnest*. I read it the first time when I was a boy and my mam was a big fan of it."

I giggle. "I should have guessed. Oscar Wilde. Irish poet and playwright. Not to mention a classic. Good choice. Tell me more about you. What else don't I know?"

"I like eggs as well, though I like mine poached or over easy with toast and sausage. I'm not sure I've ever had French toast before. I'm allergic to shrimp, and if I could, I'd eat my mam's soda bread and Shepherd's pie every day. I've been living in hotels and tour buses for months and my flat in Boston is small and depressing since I'm hardly ever there. I already told ye about my mam and how I came to the States and all about my band." He cups my jaw in his large, calloused hand. "Are ye saying yer okay with what I've done?"

"I'm saying pretending you're my boyfriend isn't the worst thing. It'll hopefully keep Hunter away. But that's not the only reason I like the idea of it. What does that mean for you leaving?"

"I... I don't know. I was planning on heading home tomorrow."

"You could stay," I offer, which maybe is ridiculous. I don't know him and now we're pretending to be something we aren't. It's asking for trouble. But I want him to stay anyway. I have a crush on Cian O'Connor and even if it'll never lead to anything real, that doesn't mean I want him to go either. Plus, well, I think he's alone for Christmas and the thought of that breaks my heart. My family isn't perfect. We're a bit zany and off the walls and do Christmas way over the top, but that's better than being alone, isn't it?

"Vivian, I... I don't know."

"Think about it? I understand if you want to go home and have time for yourself. But it's a real offer and not just because you're my new fake boyfriend. Home cooking and tree decorating and mall shopping and sledding with hot chocolate after. The works. Besides, you might not have a choice now if my mother already loves you. She's very persuasive." I laugh at that before I can stop it. "How is it my mother and father know who you are, but I didn't?"

He shrugs, his thumb gliding up along my cheek, his eyes following the motion. "They're cooler than you are."

"Apparently so." I fall forward, my face planting into his chest and I take a deep inhale. Leather and fire and spice and sex. I think that pretty much sums Cian up. "So just think about it if that's something you think you'd enjoy. There's a bathroom over there." I point to my left without looking. "Bed is over there." I point in the other direction, though it's far from necessary. "I'm on top, you're on bottom."

He grunts. "I was trying very hard not to make it dirty in my mind when yer father said that."

A smile springs to my lips and I trap it between my teeth. "How's that working out for you?"

"Not so great. Especially with ye pressed up against me in the dark like this with yer childhood bed so close. But I'll manage it."

"You're very respectful."

"Doesn't mean my thoughts are."

Mine either. "You can have the bathroom first."

His hand runs down the back of my head along my hair. "Nah, you go on. I have to go through a few things in my bag. Check on my guitar."

I pry myself away from his chest before I do something

crazy like kiss him or rip off his clothes, throw him on my bed, and climb on top of him for real. My freaking panties have been a wet mess all night and that's just from his delicious smirks and crazy sexy voice and accent. The man himself does unholy things to my body and I haven't even kissed him. Yet.

Wordlessly I go to my own bag and pull out a T-shirt and shorts along with my toiletries. Entering the bathroom, I shut and lock the door behind me and stare into the mirror over my sink. Holy shit. Holy freaking shit! A bubble of incredulous laughter tries to make its way out of my chest, but I clap a hand over my mouth, stifling it.

I've never done anything like this. I've never been impulsive or reckless. I've dated two guys seriously and only slept with four total. I'm a good girl despite the smutty stuff I write. But what fun has any of that ever gotten me? Cian was jealous of Hunter, and I've seen how he's been looking at me and touching me all night.

He feels this too, or he wouldn't have claimed me as his.

So fuck it.

I'm going to ride this train till it crashes and burns in my face and then I'll pick myself up out of the ashes and be reborn like a phoenix. I have nothing to lose at this point. And hell, maybe I'll even get a story out of it. I'll keep my heart in check because I'd be stupid not to and another broken heart isn't all that appealing.

I can do this.

It might even be fun.

Pep talk down, I pee, wash my face, brush my teeth, and apply face cream, and holy shit, there is a hot rock star in my childhood bedroom right now. I do another freak-out. A tiny screechy scream that I muffle in my towel, and when I think I've got this under control a bit better, I clear away my stuff so Cian has room in my small bathroom, and then I open the door.

My heart leaps in my chest, instantly setting off at a sprint.

Cian is across the room, his bags open as he riffles through them but when the flash of light cuts across the floor, he twists and takes me in. His eyes find my bare legs first, gliding up so slowly it makes me want to squirm where I stand. I'm about to catch on fire from the heat he's putting off. He keeps going, up along my hips, the thin college T-shirt I'm wearing up to my nipples that I know are visibly hard all the way up to my freshly scrubbed face.

His blue eyes are dark and hooded as he emits a shaky, uneven breath.

"Fuck," he mutters so low I have to strain to hear it as he runs a hand through his sandy hair.

I clear my throat. "Bathroom is all yours."

A head nod and when he stands, I catch his attempt to hide having to adjust his dick. The thought of him being hard from looking at me sends a fresh burst of lust straight through me, tightening my already wet, achy core and making my breasts heavier, my nipples harder.

The air in the room is thick, tense with desire, and a bit of awkwardness. I move for the bed and without a word he crosses the room and goes straight into the bathroom, locking it behind him. Blowing out a breath, I climb up the ladder and under the covers, settling in on the warm flannel sheets my mother has our housekeeper put on every bed this time of year. My thoughts are anxious to scatter, to start overthinking and second-guessing, but I won't allow them.

I will myself to relax. To close my eyes and try to sleep. But it's useless, especially as I hear the shower turn on and Cian move about in the bathroom. I can't help but picture him naked. His tattoos and hard muscles I've already felt a hint of through his clothes.

Is he jerking himself off in there?

If he is, is he thinking about me?

My hand slides south, over my swollen breasts and hard

nipples down into my shorts and beneath my underwear. I can't stand it a second longer, already a hot beat away from climbing down the ladder and knocking on that bathroom door.

My legs spread and I find my slick clit, swollen and pulsing, and I moan softly as I rub it. I picture Cian. I picture him sneaking his hand into my underwear and finding me wet for him. I picture him sliding my shorts down and putting his face between my thighs. Holding me down and against him with his strong grip as he French kisses my pussy. He covers my mouth with his large hand to stifle my sounds so we don't get caught. Two fingers slip inside me, his tongue flicking at my clit, and fuck, it feels so good.

Him eating me like this.

Ravenous for me.

A groan of satisfaction followed by a grunt of desire that has him fucking the bed because he's so riled up, he can't help himself.

My hand moves faster, anxious to finish myself off before Cian comes out of the bathroom. But there's a delicious naughtiness to that too. Him catching me with my hand in my pussy thinking about him. My back arches, my other hand squeezing my breast, pulling on my nipple. He whispers dirty things to me. Tells me how badly he wants to fuck me, and I come on a muffled cry when I hear the shower turn off and him step out.

A few minutes later, the door opens, and thankfully my panting has all but stopped, my body no longer ready to snap in two. Can he tell what I just did? Smell my arousal in the air? Do I even care if he does? No. I want him to ask me. I want him to know.

In the darkness of my room, my sense of hearing is heightened, and I listen intently as he climbs into the bed beneath me, smelling like soap with his hair likely wet. He shifts around and then sighs deeply, the sound both content and frustrated if that's even possible.

"Good night, Vivie Girl. Sweet dreams and happy birthday, darlin'."

"Good night, Cian."

Rolling onto my side, I close my eyes, forcing myself to sleep. But the last thought I have before I drift off is that I can't wait to see him again in the morning. And it scares me.

6

VIVIAN

When I wake the next morning, I don't have to look to already know he's not in the room. It's too quiet. No hint of his breathing, deep or otherwise. Blinding sun reflecting off the snow shines in through the window that I forgot to close the shade on, and I wonder if it woke him early.

Climbing out of bed, my suspicion is confirmed when I find his bed made. He made the bed. I'm not sure why that has me so surprised, but it does. He's such an interesting character. A rock star with a bad-boy aura about him. The way he dresses and his colorful tattoos and the accent and smirk with dimples. He's been photographed with different women a dozen times over and even caught with a couple of groupies straddling his lap.

But beneath all that, he's... a good man, I think. Different than you'd think he'd be. The way he treated that elderly woman on the plane, helping her up and into her new seat. The way he let me sleep on him without complaint. How he offered to drive me home and then came to my rescue with Hunter. How respectful he was with my father.

He seems more lost than anything. Misplaced and lonely—how could he not feel that way after all he's been through between his father and then moving to another country and then losing his mother at such a young age and then bouncing around the foster care system?

I use the bathroom and get myself dressed into warmer pajamas and then I head downstairs, already hearing the mayhem that is my family before I reach the bottom step. The smell of bacon and eggs and something sweet permeates the air, making my stomach rumble and my chest squeeze.

Home.

I needed this more than I think I realized.

Rounding the corner, I walk through the downstairs to the back of the house where the dining room is. And when I get there, I find my nieces running around the table, my sister-in-law yelling at them to stop, my brother in a heated argument with Hunter over the Patriot's last game and them hopefully making the playoffs, my father quietly reading the paper, and my mother all over Cian, piling his plate with more food than one human can eat and rapid firing him with a million different questions.

Cian glances up, noticing me and a smile cuts clear across his face, growing wider when he takes in my red pajamas that say, "#1 on Santa's Naughty List." He stands and immediately crosses the room, his eyes all over me and silence falls in the dining room, so glaring you could hear a pin drop.

"Morning, darlin'. Ye look adorable in this." He tugs on the bottom of my top and then leans in to kiss my cheek before whispering huskily in my ear, "But I think I liked what you were wearing last night more."

I feel my face flush, especially knowing everyone is staring at us, watching us intently.

"I can't believe you came down here on your own. You're

either insanely brave or didn't realize you were taking your life into your own hands."

"Ye looked so sweet sleeping, I didn't have the heart to wake ye. But now that yer here, I wouldn't mind a bit of saving. Yer brother and Hunter aren't my biggest fans though yer mother and sister-in-law certainly are."

"Oh God." I laugh, covering my face with my hands, my forehead dropping to his shoulder. "I'm so sorry."

He chuckles into me before his tone grows serious. "Nothin' to be sorry about. But at some point, we need to talk."

I nod, agreeing with him, even as my heart picks up a few extra anxious beats.

But as Hazel rips Cian away from me and envelops me in a huge hug followed by my nieces, Peter, and unfortunately even Hunter, it seems that talk is going to have to wait.

"You're home," my mother cries, stealing me from Hunter and dragging me straight into her arms. "I'm so happy you're finally home. Though why you didn't immediately come home after you left Harry is beyond me. What an ass he turned out to be. And besides, who names their child Harry?"

"Diana and Charles?"

My mother rolls her eyes at Peter. "Well, this Harry is certainly not a prince. He was nothing more than a Harry ass. Or a Harry wart. On his Harry ass." She laughs hysterically at her own joke.

"Grandma said ass," Willow, one of my almost five-year-old twin nieces, exclaims in a tattletale voice.

"We talked about how when Grandma is around, you can't listen or repeat the bad words that she says," Hazel reminds her, picking Willow up and walking her back over to the table to sit down.

Cian snickers, coughing into his arm.

"You didn't warn him about me," my mother accuses,

pointing to Cian though she's glowing brighter than her red hair—dyed at this point though once natural like mine.

"He likely wouldn't have come if I did," I quip, and she smacks at my arm before hugging me again.

"Oh, hush up. We missed you and I know you missed us."

"I did miss you." I hug her back fiercely.

"Happy birthday. I'm so sorry we didn't get to celebrate it last night, but we'll do cake tonight."

"Let the girl breathe, Darla," my father says dryly without bothering to glance up from his paper. He already has a pencil behind his ear for the crossword puzzle when he gets to it.

"I'm emotional, Theo. All of my children are home. I can't help it." My mother releases me, wiping at her face.

"Do I count as one of your children?" Hunter asks, shoveling a forkful of French toast—barf—into his mouth.

My mother says, "Yes," while my father says, "No."

"If you were one of their children, you couldn't marry Viv," Peter chimes in.

"He's not marrying her," my father says while I reply with something similar.

"Well, certainly not now that she has Cian as her boyfriend," my mother simpers, patting Cian on the face like he's a small boy.

"Couldn't agree more." Cian takes my hand and leads me to the dining room table ladened with enough food to feed the entire town. He sits me beside him—resting his hand on my thigh as if it's the most natural position for it—on the side farthest from Hunter who is visibly scowling at us while mindlessly shifting food around his plate. I have no idea why Peter felt the need to drag him along. Peter knows what happened between us.

In fact, the two didn't talk for a while.

Because what Hunter did was not only break up with me when I thought he was going to propose, but then he fucked not one but two sorority girls at a big frat graduation party the next night when he knew I was there. Why? I don't know. To prove to me that I didn't matter to him anymore? Whatever. I was wrecked. It hurt like nothing ever had. Three years of my life—my entire college life at Yale up to that point—with him and that's what he did to me.

So he can scowl and glare all he wants.

I didn't invite him, and I owe him nothing.

"Do ye want scrambled eggs, Vivie?" Cian asks me, calling my attention back to him and obviously recalling our conversation from last night. He gives me a small, amused smile that makes his dimples sink in and my mother audibly sighs like she's watching a Hallmark movie.

I don't know what he's still doing here either. By all accounts he should be gone. The snow has stopped, and the roads are plowed. But here he sits wearing jeans, a deep-blue sweater that does wild and enticing things to his eyes, and a smile that feels like it's just for me.

It's an act. I know it is. But I have no idea what he gets out of any of this.

"Eggs would be great. Thanks."

Cian takes my plate and goes about filling it up with some of everything on the table minus the French toast and damn him. I don't know if this is part of the show or him being a totally freaking nice and considerate guy, but no one has ever done this for me before.

"So now she can't make her own plate?"

My mother hisses over at Peter who's scowling equally as hard as Hunter.

"Hush it, Peter," my mother snaps. "Look how he dotes on her. So sweet. Haven't you heard his ballads? They're all about love." Another audible sigh as my mother practically leans all over Cian, her red hair tickling the edge of his shoulder.

"You owe me a hundred bucks," my father muses, setting

the paper down flat on the table and removing the pencil from behind his ear.

"I never took that bet."

He shrugs as if that small detail is irrelevant. "But I was right all the same. She hasn't let Cian breathe for a moment. Though I will say he's been an exceedingly good sport about it."

"What's all this about?" my mother asks.

"Nothing," my father and I say in unison.

"Vivian, how could you have not told us you were dating Cian O'Connor?" My mother picks up. "Or that you were bringing him home for Christmas?" She turns to him, clinging far too close for normal human boundaries' sake. "Not that we're upset about that at all, because we're not, and as I've already told you, you have to stay until you leave for your next tour."

Oh Jesus.

"Mom, Cian has a place in Boston he was thinking of—"

"Mrs. Scott, while I am still very grateful for the invitation, Vivian didn't want to impose me on yer family Christmas, and I'd hate to do the same."

"So don't—"

My mother cuts Hunter off instantly. "You're one-hundred-percent welcome here for as long as you'd like. We'd love you to stay with us through the holiday. Wouldn't we, Theo?"

My father lifts his head. "Huh? Oh, yeah. Sure." Then he returns to the paper, scribbling down an answer to something.

"See," my mother continues as if that's proof positive. "Plus, I know Vivian would love it too."

I twist to him, attempting to read Cian's face, but it's like a maximum-security prison, locked down. I open my mouth to tell him that yes, I would like him to stay when my other niece Penny cuts me off. "Mommy said she hoped he was staying too and that he'd play for us. She said he was hot, but he doesn't look like sick. Mommy always tells me I'm hot when I have a fever."

"Penny!" Hazel hisses, turning as red as the stockings hanging over the fireplace.

"You did. We heard you telling Grandma that in the kitchen," Willow pipes in, her expression curious and innocent.

"You said you think he's hot?" Peter grumbles, pointing a finger at Cian while staring daggers into Hazel.

"Well, I mean, I didn't... he is... but you know..." She sighs in defeat, covering her face with her hands. "He's a famous rock star, Peter. What do you expect?"

"For my wife not to think my sister's boyfriend is hot. But wait. You're actually dating my sister? *My sister*? How on earth did *that* happen? You two couldn't be any more different," Peter snaps at Cian, even more agitated than he was a few minutes ago.

"Don't look so shocked." I fork a piece of eggs and shove it into my mouth. "We met at a bar and started talking. I had no clue who he was other than an impossible flirt, but we just clicked. And besides, opposites with similar interests attract."

"Is this fodder for one of your books?"

I groan, rolling my eyes. "No. I write athletes, Peter. Not rock stars. You know this already because you used to make fun of it." I take a sip of some much-needed coffee before downing half of my mug. Burn to the tongue be damned.

"But seriously," Hunter chimes in. "Are we supposed to believe you're not nailing groupies while you're dating her?"

"Zip it, Hunter," I bark. "You have no right to—"

Cian covers my hand with his on the table, cutting me off. He stares at me with a soft smile as he answers Hunter. "No, I'm not. Since the moment I met Vivian, I haven't so much as looked at another woman."

I try to hide my snicker and nearly choke on my eggs

because no, he hasn't. But it's of course only been half a day since we met.

He turns to Peter first and then Hunter. "But truthfully, I haven't dated anyone in a bit due to my recording and traveling schedule, so any pictures you've seen of me online with other women are of me when I was single. Most of those pictures are pure rubbish anyway with not an ounce of truth to them. Now that I'm with Vivian, I'd never do anything to hurt or betray her. Ever."

More sighs, this time from Hazel and my nieces as well as my mother.

"He's dreamy," Willow says, dropping her cheek to her pressed-together hands that rest on the table. "Like Flynn Ryder or Kristoff."

"Do you even know what he's saying?" Peter asks her.

Her red pigtails fly around as she whips her head to squint at her father. "He just told you that he likes her. Like, duh, Daddy."

"How could you possibly have understood that?"

"Um. Hello. Because we understand boys better than you," Penny replies.

"Now that that's all settled, what time are we leaving to go get the tree?" my father asks, changing the subject entirely. And just like that, more loud chatter and arguing ensue.

Peter and Hunter grumble. My nieces start running around the table again as my sister-in-law yells after them to stop. My mother tells everyone we're leaving in one hour to go and pick out the tree. And the tree in our family is no joke. We fucking *Christmas Vacation* the hell out of our trees, hiking into the snow to cut down the perfect pine or fur.

I eat my breakfast with Cian's hand on my thigh the entire time, along with Hunter's murderous gaze locked on me. My mother is all over Cian, asking him about his music and what inspired what and how he thinks his third album will do. Cian takes it all in stride and by the time he and I find our way back upstairs, I'm out of breath and the food I just ingested doesn't want to be digested.

I slam the door to my bedroom shut behind us, pressing myself up against the wood, and digging the butts of my palms into my eyes. "That was awful. I'm so sorry they were all over you like that. I'd tell you my family isn't normally like that, but they are." My hands fall to my sides. "Are you okay? As much as I'd like you to stay through the holiday, if you feel the need to flee, I totally and completely get it. You wanted rest and relaxation and my family isn't giving you an inch to breathe and—what? Why are you staring at me like that?"

"Did ye mean it?"

I blink about a thousand times at him, tilting my head as I think through all that I just said. "Mean what? That you can go, and I'll understand? Of course."

"No. That you'd like me to stay."

Oh. And just that like a flush the color of molten lava stains my face. Cian takes a step in my direction and then another until he's only about a foot away, his ice-blue eyes, so bright in the morning light, are all over my face. But I can't tell by his expression what he's after. If he wants me to say yes or if he'd be relieved if I said no.

So I tell him the truth.

"I'd like that very much." I swallow nervously. "And I know I'll miss you if you go. Even though we just met, I think I already know that about you. Weird, right? I'm rambling, but only because I'm nervous. The way you're staring at me is making my heart pound in some crazy rhythm. But if you feel you need to be home for a bit before you go back on tour, I completely understand. I do and I won't be... I don't know. I know it's been a long several months without a break for you."

My voice cuts off when his hand presses to my chest right over my racing heart. He feels the thrum of it for a moment before his fingers glide up, tickling the space at the base of my neck where my aorta rises up to meet his touch up along my neck to the pulse point there.

His touch only makes my heart beat faster and when he feels that, he smiles as if this pleases him immensely. "I do make yer heart race."

"Now you're just showing off," I accuse breathily.

He inches in, his heady scent killing me slowly.

"I'd miss ye too if I left. And it doesn't feel weird or too soon, which is maybe what makes it so weird. And I like yer family, Vivie. Even if they are a bit much. But I've never had a bit much. It was always me and my mam who worked too many hours to put food on the table and then she was gone, and it was a bunch of families who didn't know me or try to get to know me or care enough to yell at me or ask questions or pile my plate with more food than I could ever eat. But most of all, I like how ye looked coming downstairs in your pajamas, all sleep rumpled and gorgeous. I like the way ye smell when I'm close to ye and I love how yer heart beats like this just fer me. Maybe it started as fierce, unshakable jealousy over Hunter and that's still there—I hate that you have a strong history with him and not one with me—but he's not the reason I'd stay. You are. So if ye want me to, I will."

With my breath trapped in my lungs, I say, "I want you to."

His eyes sparkle as they take me in, his hands gliding up along my face and into my hair. I'm asking for so much heartache it's likely going to have its own zip code when this is all done and finished.

"I don't know what this is between us," he says, looking a little pale and a ton off balance. "I can't make any promises beyond these nine days. I have a flight out of Boston on the thirtieth and I don't come back home for another four months. Even then, I was thinking about sellin' my place, because I'm mostly in LA now fer recording and I don't have much of a reason to call Boston home anymore."

"I know. I'm not expecting anything. It's not real, but for these nine days we have left, we can pretend it is."

He frowns at that but nods all the same. It's the reality of this and we can't change that. Even knowing where it's headed, I can't find it in me to stop it. I don't want Cian to be alone for Christmas. I want him here. With me. I want his eyes and his smirks that make his dimples pop. I want to flirt and touch and pretend.

And I'll do my best to hold my heart back. To tuck it in and remind it that this has a quickly approaching expiration date. Fleeting and fun.

"Maybe we should practice kissing," I offer. "You know, so it appears real."

"Probably a good idea, that. It has to look natural."

"Right. Natural. Passionate."

"Definitely passionate." His thumb is on my bottom lip. His eyes too. He inches in closer, his breath fanning across my lips. "I can't pretend to be yer man if I don't know what ye taste like."

"That would be crazy."

"Nonsensical."

"Ugh," I moan. "Such a good word."

He smirks, his body now inches from mine. "So, I'm gonna kiss ye then. Ye know, for practice and such. Or maybe, possibly for more than practice."

"More than practice?" My belly swoops.

"Vivie, I think ye already know how badly I want to kiss ye. I've wanted yer lips since the first second I saw ye."

His head dips in, his eyes holding mine, waiting to see what I'll do, and when I tilt my head and my eyes start to flutter closed, he moves in closer, his thumb dragging along my cheek. Warm, sweet breath across my lips, and just as I catch the barest hint of his lips on mine, the door pounds at my back, jarring us apart.

"We're leaving soon, and you better not be doing anything naked in there," Peter barks.

"Fuck off, Peter," I yell back, but he didn't stick around to argue. He's already down the hall in his room.

Cian pulls back, taking a few steps from me. He chuckles, but it's tense and edgy, the heat of what almost happened still heavy in the air between us. All I know is that if I kiss him now, I won't be able to stop and then there will definitely be naked things happening in here.

I clear my throat and force myself to move past him over to my suitcase. "I should shower."

He runs a hand through his hair, gripping the back of his neck. "Aye. I'll em, I'll go see if yer mam needs help cleaning up the kitchen."

With that, he's out the door, shutting it behind him, and I have no idea what we're doing or how we'll pull it off. But I do know with all this sexual tension bubbling just beneath the surface between us, it's only a matter of time before the pressure gets to be too much and we explode.

7

CIAN

My feet are numb. My bollocks are aching. My hands are twitching. And my eyes are glued to Vivian's fine arse in fucking snow pants which makes no sense in any normal part of the world but has me so wound up I'm just hoping and praying her father, brother, and fucktwat ex don't catch sight of my straining cock through my jeans. And in this cold, my cock should be tucked up tight, hiding, and begging for mercy.

Because Lord Jesus, it is cold. And we're in at least a foot of snow in the middle of nowhere. I have no idea why I'm even out here. Who goes to chop down their own Christmas tree when there are perfectly acceptable and accessible lots nearby? We passed two on our way out here alone. Last night I was hitting on a woman in a bar and today I'm acting the maggot in Connecticut with a fake girlfriend and her overbearing family instead of taking in much-needed quiet time alone in Boston.

All I know is I like this woman beyond reason.

I must, right? Why else would I agree to stay through Christmas—Christmas of all fucking holidays—or have stepped in and opened my mouth in a stormy and impulsive haze of jealousy in the first place? The way he looks at her... I grunt and her brother casts me a side-eye I readily ignore. I've lost my bloody mind on a girl I hardly know. This possessive version of me is new and has me reacting without thinking.

She's a woman I can't keep.

Even if the idea of it isn't the worst I've had. Especially when her head turns over her shoulder and she treats me to her breathtaking smile that melts all the snow and ice that's been encased around my heart, bathing me in a delicious warmth when I'm nearly positive my toes have frostbite in my boots that evidently aren't the least bit waterproof.

"You okay?" she mouths to me as she walks ahead with Hazel.

I return her smile with a goofy one of my own. "Aye," I mouth back. She winks at me and then flips her head around, her red hair flying along with her, and fuck. I'm so fucked. I haven't even kissed her. This woman has me all spun up. I met her less than twenty-four hours ago.

What the hell am I doing?

"You can stare at her ass all you like, but at the end of this when you're long gone and I'm still here, I'm going to be the one who gets to fuck it, not you."

Right. That's what the hell I'm doing. Protecting her from this cocksucker.

Reluctantly I remove my gaze from Vivian's arse up to the dark-headed man beside me. He is carrying an axe after all. "Yer only here because her brother invited ye. Not Vivian. The way I hear it, she wants nothing to do with you. Every attempt you've made to talk to her today she's brushed off."

He shrugs indifferently, his expression resigned. "She's just mad is all. I knew she was expecting me to propose to her. But I was about to graduate college and I panicked, thinking that at twenty-two Vivian would be the last pussy I'd ever have. Now five years later, I've had plenty of pussy and none have been as good as hers."

"Wow. You're a right piece of shite, aren't ye? Real fucking gentleman. Does her brother know ye have such romantic feelings for his sister?"

He laughs under his breath as if I'm ridiculous. "Peter loves Vivian and he loves me. We've been best friends since we were six. He wants Vivian and me to end up together. Why else would he have invited me to spend the holiday up here?"

"Well, you being here or not, I'm not going anywhere and Vivian is most certainly mine and not yours."

My gaze returns to Vivian, watching as she laughs and chats with her dad, Peter, and Hazel. Their twins stayed home with Vivian's mam because chopping down a tree is too dangerous for the wee ones. Who knew families did all this just for one holiday?

"You say you're not going anywhere, but I heard you tell everyone this morning how you're going on tour in Europe and have to leave before New Year's. I also know Vivian isn't returning to DC. She's a bit lost on where to move and it won't be difficult to convince her to move to New York. As an author, that's a great place to find inspiration and write, not to mention there are several large publishing houses there along with Peter, Hazel, and the girls. It's also close to her parents, so you see how perfect that would be for her."

"Ah, so yer plan is to soften her up over these two weeks. Get her to forgive ye for breaking her heart and then when she moves to New York at yours and Peter's strong suggestions, swoop in for the kill."

He gives me that smarmy grin that seems perpetually glued to his dickface mug. "Something like that. So while you're thousands of miles away fucking groupies and getting drunk and high or whatever you douchebag rock stars do, I'll be back in Vivian's bed and heart and you'll be long gone."

My frozen fists clench, as does my jaw. I could throw out a hundred different things. Talk about how I'm not going anywhere—I am in nine days. Tell him how Vivian is different—she is. Tell him how it's only four months apart and that means nothing—except it means everything.

Vivian isn't actually mine. None of this between us is real other than the way I want her and how she seemingly wants me back. I like her and I'm pretty sure she likes me too. But this attraction she feels for me will fizzle or fade or die the moment I'm gone.

I can't compete with this vision he's painted.

Everything he's saying *will* likely happen.

She'll move to New York to stay close to her family and he'll remind her of all the things she once loved about him—though I can't think of anything about this man that's endearing—and he'll win her heart over again. That will be that. Checkmate, Vivian ends up with Hunter.

So I should leave. I have no business being here. I'm risking something with this girl I've never been willing to risk with another simply because I can't seem to stop myself with her, but I need to.

Before I can formulate any sort of witty—or even not so witty—retort, a body slams into me, taking me by surprise and startling me out of my lost thoughts. Vivian's arms are draped around my shoulders, her laugh tickling my neck.

"Oh my gosh, it's freezing. I can hardly feel my face, but this tree is so perfect, right?"

"Huh?" I finally manage, blinking back and watching as Hunter stalks off toward the tree everyone is gathered around. My arms wrap around Vivian, breathing in the scent of her hair and feeling the cold of her skin against mine. For a moment, I wonder if she's hugging me because I was next to Hunter, but it's as if she didn't even realize he was here. Do I want that for her? To not ever be with him even when she can't be with me?

Is that selfish?

No. He's a rotten piece of gobshite.

"You okay?" she asks and her question throws me until I realize I'm holding on to her for dear life, practically crushing her against me.

"Grand," I lie.

She draws back, removing her glove and pressing her palm to my cheek. I shudder, burying myself against the warmth. Her nose and cheeks are rosy, her green eyes as bright as the giant tree behind her. She's a stunning vision and my heart does some sort of painful acrobatics in my chest.

"Have you ever decorated a Christmas tree before?"

I set her down, keeping her close to my side as we slowly trudge through crunchy snow and ice to join the others.

"No," I admit, staring warily at the tree as Hunter and Peter take turns at the trunk with an axe. "I haven't."

"Well, you're in for it now. In case it hasn't been obvious, we Scott's don't half-ass anything when it comes to Christmas."

"So I'm learning. Is this going to be like that movie where ye get this thing in yer house and then there's a fucking squirrel that jumps out?"

She laughs, resting her head on my arm. "No. Definitely not. That only happened once, and it was a chipmunk. Not a squirrel." Her smile is unstoppable when she reads the horrified look on my face. "I'm kidding. That never happened. No woodland creatures will jump out of this tree."

I sure as hell hope not.

TWO HOURS later after a lot of chopping and dragging a tree that had to weigh at least a ton and sweating despite the subfreezing temperatures we're sitting around the living room by the fire enjoying hot apple cider with a healthy splash of whiskey in it. Mr. Scott, who has insisted I call him Theo along with Peter, managed the massive tree into the water basin and now has the thing upright in the corner. Everyone is sort of sprawled about the room, quiet and wrecked.

The house smells like whatever wonderful roast Darla is cooking and in the background is the faint hum of Christmas music and whatever children's program the girls are watching in the back room.

Vivian is sitting on my lap, snuggled in, enjoying her drink while staring into the fire. My fingers play absently with her hair, both of us lost in a sleepy sort of lull after the hours spent in the cold. Boxes of lights and Christmas ornaments sit in front of the tree, waiting to be opened and sorted and placed in the perfect spot. Evidently that's typically done after dinner along with a lot of alcohol.

Outside snow has started to fall again, the sun already set.

Vivian yawns just as her stomach grumbles, making her giggle against me. "I think I can officially say that whiskey makes me tired."

I grin into her hair, kissing the top of her head. "Aye, but you're adorable when ye sleep on me so I won't complain about it."

She tilts her head back, meeting my eyes. "Good. Because I certainly wouldn't mind sleeping on you later."

My cock instantly stirs beneath her and when she feels it against her arse she smiles and wiggles into it.

"Is that a fact?" My fingers trickle along her cheek, my eyes flickering about her face.

She leans in and whispers, "I don't even care if you're on bottom and I'm on top. I like sleeping in all kinds of positions."

I suppress a groan, quickly peeking about the room. Peter and Theo appear to be half-asleep and not paying us any attention at all. It's certainly not the ideal place for our first kiss, but with her against me, saying these dirty words, I have to. I have to steal one taste.

"Woman, ye have no idea all the things I want to do to ye." My lips skirt along hers, a tickle that shoots like electricity through my body. I pull back and tilt my head the other way, a ravenous hum of pleasure escaping my throat as I thrill along her again without pressing in. It's a simple brushing, but so good.

"More," she whispers into me, and I can't deny her.

I set my mug down and cup the back of her head, my lips drawing down on hers when Hunter comes rushing into the room. "The roast is on fire," he yells seconds before the fire alarm blares and everyone bolts up, screaming and yelling and running for the kitchen that is now funneling plumes of acrid gray smoke into the rest of the house.

Vivian flies off my lap, running to help put out the fire, and as I stand, I catch Hunter's satisfied grin. Fucker did that on purpose. Only now that I've had the smallest of tastes it'll take a hell of a lot more than a simple fire to keep me away from Vivian. He wants a fight, he's got one coming.

8

VIVIAN

I should feel guilty about lying to my family. Especially when I've never lied to them about anything before. Vivian, the good girl. Vivian, the dependable one. Vivian, the author who writes some serious smut but is successful at it. But really, all I've done is follow someone else's model for me.

I went to Yale because that's where my parents went. I dated Hunter because we grew up together and he was my brother's best friend. I expected him to put a ring on it because that's what the graduating boys did with their younger girlfriends if they wanted to lock them down. I became an author because my freshman college creative writing professor told me I had talent and potential and to choose a popular niche in order to be successful.

The crazy part? All of that felt seamless. Like I was making those choices for myself.

But other than loving writing romance, have I done any of that?

I don't think so.

Maybe that's why this lie feels so good when I know it shouldn't. It's my act of teenage rebellion. I brought home an

Irish rock star for Christmas. A tattooed bad boy, sexy as all fuck rock star.

So the fact that he's actually this guy? This sweet, humble, helpful, playful, genuine, lost guy? Well, we already know it has my lady parts on high alert, but I also feel like I'm on the inside of the joke. Like I have backstage access no other woman has ever had before. He's hinted at it, but I don't think Cian has ever had a serious girlfriend before.

He's certainly never been photographed with the same woman twice.

And even though I'm not a serious girlfriend or even a real girlfriend to him, he's here pretending that I am. Me! And I'm not even being self-deprecating. But I'm a regular girl just the same. A girl from Connecticut with an Ivy League education and a slightly off-the-wall family.

Which is why the question begs asking. Why?

Why is Cian here? Why is he staying? Especially when we know we're not headed anywhere.

But in moments like these, it's impossible to question him. It's also impossible to beat my brain and heart back into submission when the man is crooning in my ear in that sexy as all sin voice, singing lyrics to songs I've never heard before as we dance around each other in the kitchen, cleaning up after the nearly ruined roast and birthday cake with my family.

He loads up the last dish into the dishwasher and I toss him a pod that he puts in the slot and then starts it up. I have to laugh at that, and he throws me a curious look.

"Do all rock stars do the dishes?"

He gives me a goofy grin. "When they're still trying to impress their woman, they do."

In a flash, he crosses the kitchen and wraps his arms around my waist, dipping me back a little. The heat of his body presses against mine and I'm so desperate for him to kiss me I'm practically pulsing with the need of it.

But he doesn't kiss me. He gets within inches of my mouth and freezes there. "I never got to properly celebrate yer birthday."

"My birthday?"

His nose tickles along mine. "Yer birthday. I never got to do anything for it. How about I take you out tonight? We'll find a bar and go dancing."

"Dancing?"

"Are ye just going to repeat my words back to me?"

"When they start making sense I won't."

He chuckles, the sound vibrating into me. "I want to take ye out on a date. I want to spend some time with just you."

"Okay," I tell him because I like the way that races through my blood like a girlish flutter of a crush asking me out. "Let's do it. Tomorrow night?"

"Tomorrow night."

And it sounds like a promise. A dirty promise. The way the words hang thick and heavy and filled with want. As if reading my thoughts, he walks me backward until I'm pressed against the counter, his body caging me in. He glances around, checking both exits to make sure we're alone, and then he turns back to me.

"I can't wait another second." Then his lips slam down on mine. The gentle brushing of earlier gone as he doesn't hesitate before spreading my lips open with his and diving in. One hand slices through my hair, holding the back of my head, the other is low around my waist, pinning me to him so I feel every hard inch. So I feel just how crazy he is with need for me.

I match his ardor, moaning softly into his mouth as his tongue sweeps along mine. My hands go wild. Gripping at his hair and tugging on his shirt and grasping his strong shoulders and arms. He tastes like the chocolate of my cake and smells of fire and leather and kisses me so deeply and so thoroughly I'm dizzy with it. Drunk on how good this feels.

I assumed a man who can sing the way he can knows how to work his mouth and tongue and I wasn't wrong. I've never been kissed like this. Like he's trying to steal all the air from my lungs and infuse them with his own. His head tilts the other way, nipping at my lips, first top then bottom, groaning as he licks them, and then plunges back in. His tongue swirls with mine, deep, pulling kisses followed by sweet, soft ones.

"Woman, ye taste like the sweetest heaven and feel like the dirtiest sin." It's a growl of lust as he thrusts against me.

His hand squeezes my ass, sliding down my thigh like he's about to lift it and put it around his hip when someone sharply clears their throat. Like being shot out of a cannon, we shoot apart, both of us panting, my lips wet and swollen and his hair an absolute tussled disaster from my hands. My hands grip the counter behind me, so I don't collapse to the floor in a puddle.

"Wow." Hazel is red as she fans her face. "That was seriously hot and normally I wouldn't have interrupted that, but your dad told me to check on you because it's time for brandy and tree decorating." She throws a pointed eyebrow that says lucky for you it was me who found you and not your father. Or brother for that matter.

I give her a sheepish yet grateful smile. "We'll be right there."

With a skip in her step, she spins around, and leaves.

"Well, that almost got out of hand." Cian runs his fingers through his hair, trying to fix it.

"Almost," I murmur, suddenly feeling shy for reasons I don't quite comprehend.

He takes my hand, tugging me into him, his blue eyes dark. "I was about to hoist ye up on the countertop and have my way with ye right here in the kitchen."

"I think I would have let you."

"Then I guess it's a good thing it was Hazel who found us and not yer da or I'd be out on my arse." A smirk that makes his dimple sink into his cheek before his face grows serious. "I'm starting to get selfish with ye, Vivie. I feel like time is already getting away from us and we just got here."

"I know." That's how it feels for me too. I wish I could slow or stop time. I wish he wasn't leaving for four months. I wish he wasn't famous and had women crawling all over him wherever he went. I wish I had met him for real and this was real because I want it to be. Being with him feels so natural. So *right*.

"I want more of ye. Does that make me a total fuckin' wanker?"

"No. I want more of you too."

Since we seem to do the honesty thing. Like falling on a sword, it's both sacrificial and poetically beautiful while sucking in real life. This is why people lie. It's called self-preservation for a reason and it's a concept I never fully grasped until this moment where honesty will end up destroying me.

But thinking this way won't lead to anything good so I step out of his arms and take his hand. Plastering on a smile I don't quite feel, I lead him back out into the family room. My family and Hunter are all around the Christmas tree. My father's bottle of his favorite brandy already out along with glasses for everyone, minus Penny and Willow who are already whining about getting to be the one to put the star up on top.

Cian's chin hits my shoulder, and he drags me back a step, tucking me in and just holding me here for a moment as we watch everyone be... well... my family.

"What happens if I want to put on the star?"

I smile, knowing he can't see it. "Then I think you've got a solid fight on your hands. Don't let those cute red pigtails fool you. Redheads fight dirty and to the death."

"Ah, a man can only hope that's true. Alright. I'm about to break all the rules."

"What—"

"First little lady to climb on my back gets to put the star on the top," he calls out.

Cian pulls away from me as girlish shrieks pierce the air. Willow and Penny go sprinting over to him, both launching themselves at him and climbing up, one on each side like he's a tree.

"Hold on there, girls. Yer mam will have my neck if I drop ye." Each of his arms clutches one of the girls to his side and then he's rising to his full height, winking at Hazel and even Peter. "I realize this star is supposed to come last, but what if these ladies place it on top together now to start this all off? But only if they're willing to do it together, yeah?"

"We are! We will! Yes!" my nieces cry, bouncing on his sides as he holds them strongly up in the air.

"Alright," Peter relents. "Here's the star. But together, girls, and then we'll do the rest of the tree."

The shining gold star finds its way to my nieces' hands and as one with the help of Cian lifting their little bodies up as high as he can, they place the star at the top.

"Tell me you're not in love," Hazel whispers conspiratorially, handing me a very full tumbler of brandy that I gratefully accept.

I scoff. "I can't be, It's too soon."

She scoffs mockingly in return without removing her eyes from my fake boyfriend helping her girls put the star on top of the tree. "Who the hell ever set a time constraint on falling in love? I knew the night I met your grump of a brother that he was the one I'd marry. I was a freshman in college, and I don't regret any of it. Not getting pregnant before we were ready or walking down the aisle or him being the only man I've ever been with."

"You're talking about Peter, right?"

She laughs, smacking my arm. "Yes. I'm talking about Peter. He's just annoyed you no longer want to marry his best friend.

He'll get over it. So yeah, you could totally love Cian and it would be totally okay if you did."

I shake my head. "Not really. He's leaving for tour soon and—"

"Worships you? Yes, I know. I can see that as can your parents. Even Peter does, much to his chagrin. If Cian didn't love you, why else would he be here with you now, spoiling your nieces while settling a fight and kissing you crazy in your parents' kitchen because he knows he can't do it in your bedroom since your father laid that smackdown and he's being respectful?"

"I… I…" I fall silent.

Because I haven't found a good explanation for why Cian is here, lying that he's my boyfriend, and spending Christmas with a stranger and her family. Except maybe that he's lonely, but is that a solid reason for all of this? I pause, watching him with my nieces, smiling as he tickles and teases them, and they ruffle his hair.

Is everything she's saying true?

And fuck, just the thought that it could be sets my heart aflame.

But… no. Love isn't the right word for any of this. It's been a freaking day. One day. One hell of a day and yes, Cian feels inherently different and more natural to me than any other guy I've been with. But maybe that's Christmas. Or the close proximity of all this. Maybe that's just our chemistry—burn hot and fast and die out just as hard.

"I don't want to think about it," I tell her honestly. "I just want to enjoy this for what it is while I can enjoy it."

And with that declaration, with me forcing that somewhat bitter pill down my throat, I leave my sister-in-law and go join my fake boyfriend as he makes my nieces fall helplessly in love with him. All girlish swoons and simpering sighs and delighted squeals. He tosses them about and sets them down, telling them he needs their help with picking out the perfect ornaments.

I sit beside him on the floor, and he smiles at me, leaning in to kiss my cheek as if it's the most natural thing in the world. That is until Penny and Willow fight over who gets to sit on his lap and manage to accidentally kick him in the balls. He puffs out an *oomph*, his face scrunching up in agony as his forehead falls to my shoulder.

"Oh crap," Hazel exclaims, rushing over and attempting to pull the twins off him. "I'm so sorry. Here girls, off Cian, I think he needs a minute." She ushers them over to my mother who is entering with a plate of cookies like we didn't just have birthday cake an hour ago.

"Possibly more than a minute," Peter states, wincing in what is likely sympathy pain. "I know how precise those girls can be and when they both get you? Yeah, I don't like you because I'm obviously team Hunter, but sorry, man. I feel for you."

Cian holds his hand up in the air. "Thanks, mate." A strained grunt. "Appreciate that."

"Here, Cian. Let me top off your brandy," my father offers, filling his snifter practically to the top with amber liquid. "That'll help. Drink that and in less than five minutes, you'll forget all about your aching balls."

"Right. Thanks for that, sir." More grunting.

"Having fun?" I tease.

"That was brutal." He's still breathing hard. "Not one but two kicks. I feel like my bollocks and stomach are trying to eject themselves from my body."

I can't help my giggle.

"Ye find that funny, woman?" He nips at my shoulder. "Me in pain like this amuses ye?"

"It certainly amuses me," Hunter comments dryly, standing beside us so he can put up an ornament on the tree. One he bought me our first Christmas together. "Remember when I gave you this, Viv? It was the night I told you I loved you for the first time. If memory serves you cried the words back to me."

My eyes narrow at Hunter and Cian grunts again, his face still on my shoulder. "Bloody grand. Another direct shot to the bollocks."

"Funny," I muse, still glaring at Hunter who really should have left already. "It's so hard to remember anything from that long ago when I was so young."

Cian sits up, guzzles down half his brandy and then returns his face to my shoulder, only this time he nuzzles in on me.

"Alright," my mother exclaims. "Enough of that nonsense. This tree won't decorate itself. Vivian, up with you. I need help with the tinsel and you're behind one drink already. Theo, fill her up. This is a big tree you brought home."

"When I'm too drunk to see straight, will you carry me upstairs?"

Cian kisses the skin just beneath my ear.

"Absolutely. Then ye can sleep on me some more."

"And rub your aching balls back to health."

He hisses. "Devil woman." Another kiss and then he takes a deep inhale. "Fuck, I love how ye smell." One last kiss then he pries himself away, shifting to stand and taking my hand in one of his, his drink in his other. "Okay, my wee wan, teach me how to decorate a Christmas tree."

9

CIAN

There is no safe place here. Everywhere I go, I'm surrounded. Or trapped. My mind is spinning. My thoughts are swirling. And I have a need so great I can hardly breathe past it burning a hole through me. I haven't been able to fall asleep despite the brandy corroding my stomach lining and instead of being sleepy and reticent, I'm wired, alive, and fucking crawling out of my skin.

My eyes are plastered to the slats in the bed above me, my ears glued to Vivian's every breath. That Christmas tree downstairs is piled high with multicolored lights and about two hundred ornaments and the star on top that cost me my bollocks. After the tree was finished, the girls went down to bed, and then her parents, and then I did have to practically carry Vivie upstairs as the girl was swaying and adorably zonked with brandy.

But the words I sang to her earlier in the kitchen...

The words that were just slowly slipping in and out of my consciousness are now so loud and demanding they require more than simply writing them down—which I already did.

They require life. To be set free and given sound. A melody to live by.

Fuck.

Slipping out of bed, Vivie doesn't even so much as stir as I head for my guitar, opening the hard case and slipping my girl out. I'm hoping Vivie is too drunk to wake because Hunter is downstairs, and the rest of her family is up here and it's too fucking cold to go to the car or sit outside.

The bathroom door shuts with a small creek and then I flip on the light, taking in the small room and deciding where best to sit. The toilet seems to be my only real option, so I drop my notebook on the sink counter beside it, shut the lid of the toilet, and get into position. My fingers are already burning with a fire that has only one way of snuffing it out.

I haven't felt like this in months. And it doesn't take a genius to know the source.

Vivie.

Gorgeous redheaded girl is filling my head with lyrics.

My muse.

Opening up my notebook to the page I was working on earlier, I scribble out a few more lines as fast as my hand will carry me. The words don't stop. Flowing effortlessly like water off a cliff, I don't slow down until I have the very beginning of a full song. No agonizing over word choices or if the sounds will match up.

I nearly laugh, beyond incredulous.

It's never this easy.

Writing a song takes days, weeks sometimes.

Not tonight it seems.

Going back up to the top, I place my fingers on the frets of my guitar and then use my right hand to pluck the strings. I could use my pick, but I want to tease this out a bit first. Find the right way I want her to sound.

I sing a few measures, my voice low, a gentle hum barely above a whisper.

The moment you say the hard yes instead of the easy no.
The moment you decide to let it all go.
The moment you take your life in your own hands.
Dreams become reality no love can withstand.
The ticking of a clock. The beating of a heart.
Darlin' there is no other place to start.
The touch of your lips. The rush of my blood.
Will we ever survive this flood?
Cause I was born when your eyes met mine.
Now we're already running out of time.
But when the stars cross it's already too late.
One slip of your tongue has sealed my fate.

I pause here, letting my fingers rest on the G, my head bowed. Fuck, I don't even know what I just played. This is not how I do this. Not how I write a song and I was too wound up to remember to bring my phone in to record it. Shite. I need to get my phone, there is just no other way right now.

Pulling the strap from around my neck, I set my guitar down on the floor and flick off the light. I'm momentarily blind, my eyes unadjusted, and when I think I can make it safely to find my phone without stumbling and killing myself, I crack the door open only to slam straight into someone, toppling her back as I fall on top of her.

My hands shoot out at the last minute, one beneath her the other outstretched to try and break our fall, but we land in a pile with a heavy thud and an *oomph* from both of us.

"Shite! Vivie, ye okay?" Her head narrowly missed the side of her dresser and now we're a pile of limbs. I start to pull back, so I don't crush her and to make sure she's okay when she grabs my shirt and tugs me back down to her. My elbows brace on either side of her head as I try to see her face in the dark.

"Hi," she whispers.

I grin. "Hi. Ye okay?"

"Better now actually."

"Yeah? How's that?"

"That's the song you were singing to me earlier tonight, right?"

"Aye. Sorry if I woke ye."

She plows past my apology, her green eyes glimmering in whatever ambient light is filtering in through the window. "Is it about me?"

"Yes. Does that bother you?"

Her hands thread up into my hair, her warm, stunning curves and soft body so sweet beneath mine. "No. I'm..." She licks her lips, and my cock thickens between us, barely held back by my briefs and flimsy sleep pants. "I like it."

"But?" I question because it sounds like there's a but on the end.

"I'm trying very hard not to think of the but."

I sigh, sagging a bit deeper into her. "Me too."

"I'm starting to like you." She says it as a warning, but everything in me short-circuits with that admission. Because liking her is what I've done since the second I saw her.

"I like ye too. More than I know I should. I can't get enough of ye, woman. Do ye want me to go? Would that make it easier?"

"No," she says quickly, her warm breath against my lips. "I think that would make it harder." Her fingers rake through my hair, along my scalp and I suppress a groan at how good that feels. "This is crazy and quick, but if we stop, I'll regret it always. Let's live in the moment until we can't any longer."

I smile against her, grinding up into the *V* between her thighs, making her full lips part on a silent moan. "I like that line. Can I steal it?"

"Does that mean I get royalties or just credit? The song is about me after all."

I chuckle softly. "Credit. Ye get all the credit."

"Deal." Her grip in my hair tightens and then her lips are on mine.

"Vivie," I groan dangerously into her with whatever remaining valiant part of me that is trying to knock some sense into me. "Yer da—"

"Is asleep so you need to be quiet."

"But I don't want to disrespect—"

"Would it help if I was on top, and you were on bottom?"

Now there is no stopping my groan. Or the way my body unconsciously grinds down into her, our bodies a perfect fit.

She holds me tightly against her, her mouth moving with mine, her taste driving me mad with desire. "Please, Cian," she begs. "I want this so badly with you. I can't go the next however many days without being with you like this."

"Christ, I want ye like I've never wanted another woman."

"Then don't hold back. You sang it. Ticking clock."

She's right. As much as I like and respect her da, I can't give up this chance to be with her. Besides, there is no denying the lust swirling through me at caging this beautiful woman to the floor in such a primal, dominating way. Her thighs rub together, and the softest noise comes from the back of her throat. All other thoughts flee my mind but her.

There is no being in her parents' house. There is no me leaving in a little more than a week. There is no Hunter or anyone else. There is only her, this woman with a need so great it matches mine. A need I can satisfy for both of us.

I have to taste her. I have to touch her.

I've thought of little else since I saw her.

Like Romeo, I was bewitched and besotted from the first sight of her. Then she opened her mouth, and I haven't been able to tear myself away since.

My hands glide down the sides of her, slithering along her breasts, all the while my mouth feasts on hers. Sucking, licking, eating at her the way I plan to eat at her pussy. Just the thought of that already has my bollocks drawing up on me and if I'm not careful, this woman who feels like the prize of a lifetime, will have me coming in seconds.

Anxious fingers curl around the hem of her thin nightshirt and then I'm ripping it up and over her head. And fuck. Just *fuck*. She is *stunning*. Her tits are made for my hands, her nipples a deep rose and hard, eager for my mouth. I don't deny them. My lips and tongue attack each nipple with the same voracious eagerness I did her mouth.

I can smell her. Taste her skin. Like soap and woman and something so delicate and lovely I groan. Her hands capture my hair, holding me against her, her back arching, thrusting her tits up farther into my mouth. Sounds are tumbling from her lips, one after the other as she moves and thrashes.

"Cian, I'm going to come," she rasps and for a moment, I'm beyond surprised. Then ready to pat myself on the back for being a god and thinking I'm about to make my girl come just from licking her tits when I take a second to realize I've been grinding and dry fucking her like a madman this entire time, right on her sweet spot between her thighs.

No wonder I was so close to blowing my load already.

I'm like a dog in heat or a teenage boy with no control, but she's not complaining one bit.

"Fuck, Vivie, I have to taste that. I need to feel ye come."

I tear myself away, make quick work of stripping her out of her pajama pants, and then I toss her thighs over my shoulder and take in the beautiful sight before me. Wet. So wet. Glistening and wanting. I can't stop myself from needing to touch where my cock is so eager to go. I slip a finger inside her tight entrance, and it greets me happily, practically drawing my finger in. She moans and I feel her pussy quiver around me.

"Yer so very, very wet, darlin'."

"Cian," she whimpers. "Please."

I lean in and give her pussy a long lick and groan. Her taste and smell are what every man hungers for and now it's mine for the having. The thought makes me savage, riled up beyond rational thought. One taste will never be enough.

"What do ye need, Vivie. Tell me." I blow cool air on her and her back arches, her hands ripping at my hair as she tries to drag me back into her. "Ye want me to lick your sweet pussy? Make ye come all over my face? Hold you down and smack yer tits while I take ye with my cock?"

"Yes! Oh god, yes! All of it. Smack me, fuck me, choke me, lick me, I don't care. I want it all. Just give it to me."

Motherfucker, she's my absolute dream.

Her head pops up, her dark, hazy eyes clinging desperately to mine. "I've written it all, but I haven't experienced it all."

A rush of male confidence and ego swarm through me. "Woman, yer going to have to be the one to tell me to stop. Because I don't want to stop. I don't want to slow down. I want to do everything there is to do because I only have nine days and I can't handle that. I fucking can't. I need more time and I don't have it. So I'm going to wreck yer body, darlin'. I'm greedy like that. I want it to be mine and I want to ruin ye for all other men after me. Starting now."

With my hands holding the globes of her ass, I lick a line from her opening up to her clit where I flatten my tongue and press it firmly against her. My tongue massages her clit before I dive back down, stealing another taste of her dripping wetness. She's so messy and it's all from me and never in my life have I wanted to make a woman come more than I want to send Vivie flying to the stars. I circle her clit again, flicking it, playing, teasing enough to get her close but not over the edge.

She wiggles and writhes, her noises muffled as to not wake anyone up, but her sounds have me eating at her like a man possessed. My cock so hard it's painful.

My finger circles the rim of her entrance before sliding back in. She bucks against me and then I add a second finger, crooking them so I find her sweet spot inside. My lips circle her clit and when I suck it in my mouth, my fingers rubbing her from the inside, she detonates. Her legs lock around my head, holding me tightly against her in a ninja-like grip that makes me chuckle into her. That vibration only makes her squeeze harder, her cry just the tiniest bit louder.

Finally when the last of her spasms ebb so does the grip of her legs and she sags back into the carpet. An airy laugh breathes past her lips. "Wow."

I grin, climbing slowly up her body, kissing and licking her delicious skin as I go. My face buries in her neck and her fingers toy with my hair, combing through the thick strands. For a moment I just rest here, breathing in the scent of her skin and feeling her warm body against me as her nails drag along my scalp. A shudder racks through me that has nothing to do with the burning lust still blazing a path through me.

It's something else entirely and it quickens my pulse.

Contentment. Rapture. Peace. Home.

And fuck, in my twenty-eight years, I've never come anywhere close to any of that. I've known this woman such a short time, but it's as if my body, my mind, my heart have found where they've always been meant to be. The person they were always meant to belong to. And with that wild, rapacious, terrifying thought, I lift her thigh and hitch it around my hips. Drag my pants off my body and thrust inside my girl.

My breath rushes out in a whoosh as blinding white light flashes behind my eyes.

"Oh. Ah. Jesus. Cian, don't move."

I pull back, my brows creased. "What's wrong? Did I hurt ye?"

"No. You're just... um... big. I wasn't... you know, expecting that."

I chuckle before I can help it, dipping down so I can kiss

her. "I'm sorry. I think I lost a bit of control. Yer tighter than a fist and feel like heaven. Tell me when I can move."

"Maybe for the first time I *should* be on top."

I nip at her bottom lip, my smile matching hers, utterly uncontainable. "Probably right with that. If anyone's to get rug burn on their arse, it should be me."

She giggles, her body relaxing around me.

"Hold on tight." My hand snakes under her, flattening against her lower back, and then I roll us so she is in fact on top and I'm not sure why I didn't think of this before. She's a vision. Messy red hair and flushed face and parted lips and full tits and smooth stomach bleeding into curved hips.

She sinks down on me, slowly, testing, taking me in and the pace and feel of her are nearly the death of me. The primal need to thrust up into her is so overwhelming I have to bite my lip.

"You're not wearing a condom."

Fuck. She's right. My need to be inside her, deeper and more connected knocked my better sense from me. No wonder she feels so fucking good. "Shite. I'm doing this all wrong. I can go grab one in my bag. I've never gone bare before. I'm sorry, I wasn't thinking."

"You've never gone bare?"

I pant out a wheezing breath when she's finally all the way seated. "No. Never. I was tested about six weeks ago and I haven't been with anyone since that."

"I was tested after I ended it with my ex. I'm clean too. And I'm on the pill."

Fuck. "Vivie—"

Only I'm cut off when she rises up and then slides back down on me, taking me in deeper. A low, growly moan escapes the back of my throat.

"I'm not stopping," she warns me before she does it again, this time rocking herself forward, so her clit hits my pelvic bone. Crackles of light dance around the edges of my vision, and I grip her hips, finally allowing myself to move inside her.

Our bodies meet at the perfect moment and her head flies back, more of those hymn-like sounds she makes filling the air. She's music. My muse.

This is more than sex or lust. This is real and raw and pure. This is a woman I am bare with more than just physically. I'm emotionally tied to her in a way that flays my heart wide open.

My grip turns bruising as I thrust up into her. Her tits bounce along with her body. Skin slapping against skin, wet and noisy combined with our grunts and groans and moans. Words tumble from both our lips as I ram up into her. *Harder* and *I'm so close* and *you feel so good* and *I need it deeper* and *I can't get deep enough*. Lyrics spin and words dance as we fuck each other in perfect synchrony.

Perfect. That's the word that sticks the hardest. Everything about her is perfect. Her feel and smell and taste and the way she takes me. I fuck her like a man possessed. A wild, primal being. The idea of filling her with my cum, of feeling her cum on me has me moving us again. This time I sit up, pressing our bodies together and moving up onto my knees with her around me.

The carpet chafes at my knees and shins but it's not enough of a deterrent to have us stop or even move to the bed. Her fingernails gouge at my back, her lips sloppy as they kiss at mine. She bucks, crying out a sound that's far too loud. I grip the back of her head and plant her face into my chest as I continue to pump and thrust up, over and over and over again. I can't stop. There is no end. Even as my balls draw up and I feel the first suggestions of her orgasm as her body begins to convulse and squeeze me tighter.

"Fuck," she hisses into me, her nails digging deeper. I feel her tighten and then she's crying out again. My lips violently fuse with hers as I fuck her through her orgasm and then mine's right there. With one last stab I come, feeling every pulse of my dick as I shoot myself inside her, coating her walls and leaking onto my thighs beneath her ass.

The two of us tumble back, her sweaty body sticking to my own as we catch our breaths. My fingers glide through her hair, my lips planted on her forehead.

"Will it feed your rock star ego if I tell you that was the best sex of my life?" She blows out a heavy breath. "Though I bet you're used to hearing that."

The vulnerability in her voice tears at my soul. Cupping her face in my hand, I tilt her so her eyes are forced to meet mine. "Vivian, that was the best sex of *my* life. Hands down, no contest. This is different and special because yer both of those things to me. I'm crazy about ye, darlin'."

"But Cian—"

I shake my head and cut off her practical words and thoughts with a searing kiss. "Not yet, okay? We've got this time and I don't want to think about what happens after it."

She nods, but it's there in her eyes. Because we both know there will be an after. There is no stopping that. And it's going to hurt like hell.

10

VIVIAN

I wake up feeling like I got fucked on the floor last night. My body is sore. My lower back is aching. I'm positive I have rug burns in places one should never get rug burn. Cian and I had another round on the floor last night only to finish it all off with a third in the shower.

The man is insatiable. And big. And seriously loves giving me orgasms, which sounds wonderful and hot—and it is—but my body is most certainly paying the price for it all now.

Slowly I sit up, trying to twist and stretch out my tight muscles and then I flip my head over the side of the bed. Cian is sleeping heavily, his full lips parted with his slow, even breaths. For a moment, I watch him as I think. What started off as something impulsive is quickly turning into something else. Something that feels far too real when it never can be.

"'How quick come the reasons for approving what we like.'"

Yeah, Jane really knew how to say it. Because just yesterday morning I was filling my head with all the ways I was going to keep Cian out. Now look at me.

Let's just hope she was also right when she wrote, "When pain is over, the remembrance of it often becomes a pleasure."

Sitting back up, I creep down the ladder and sneak into the bathroom, blowing out the breath I was holding as I shut the door. I nearly jolt back in fear when I catch my reflection in the mirror. My hair is a wild, tangled mass of red on top of my head. My face is blotchy. My arms have bruises and rug burns.

Awesome.

Shaking my head at myself, I pee, brush my teeth, and start the water for the shower.

Today Hazel and I are going to the mall for last-minute shopping while my parents take the girls to some kids holiday music show, and my brother and Hunter will watch football. Cian already said he has a couple of errands and things he'd like to do, which is perfect because I have to get him something for Christmas. Only I have no idea what to get him. What does one get their rock star fake boyfriend? The irony is, I don't even know him that well. I mean, I know him. I know the important stuff. But the nuances that you pick up after being with someone for a while, those I don't know.

So I'm going to have to wing it.

Stripping out of my clothes, I step into the shower, shutting the glass door behind me. Hot water hits my rug burns and I hiss at the sting of it. Still there is no denying how good it feels on my aching muscles. My mind starts building a scene. I'm supposed to be on a writing and work break. This year I went nonstop, and my editor and assistant were worried I'd start to burn out.

But that doesn't stop my mind from going. From building new worlds and characters and stories and situations. Like this one. Because I think it would be funny if the couple did it on the floor... hmmm... maybe in the locker room? No, that's nasty. Oh, in the coach's office. She'll be the coach's daughter and he'll see a picture of her with her father while they're doing it and start to freak out. But the sex will be so good, he won't be able to stop, only to realize he's covered with rug burns after. And he'll be sore AF and all the training staff will ask about it and he'll have to come up with a good lie to cover all the naughtiness he's been up to.

Warm, wet hands wrap around my waist, and I jump ten feet in the air, screaming out at the top of my lungs while simultaneously slamming into the shower wall and bumping my elbow and head.

"Shhhh," Cian hisses, his lips fusing with mine. "You'll get us caught, you will. Are ye okay? Ye'd think I was the fucking devil touching you the way you just screamed out."

"Christ," I pant, huffing and puffing into him, my forehead falling to his bare, wet chest. "I was lost in my head. I'm not supposed to be working this break. But my mind doesn't like to shut off for too long and when I start to plot out characters or a scene or a story, I get so caught up in that world that little else registers."

"Considering I said yer name twice before I came in the shower with ye, I will agree on that. I get like that when I'm writing songs. It's like all I can hear are the notes and the lyrics in my head."

"Yes!" I exclaim. "That's totally it. But for me, I see the scenes I want to write."

"That's why we both carry notebooks on us."

I look up at him, licking my lips as water runs down my face in rivulets. "We're both lost, old souls. So different and yet not."

A reluctant, sad sort of smile pierces his lips. "Why is it I'm meeting ye now?"

I don't have an answer for that. I know what he's saying. Why did we meet now when he's leaving for four months and I'm... I don't know what I am or where I'm headed even. Peter mentioned coming to New York and there is merit in that. It makes sense in so many ways, and part of me is effortlessly tempted since that was where I had always pictured myself living after college.

In fact, the only reason I didn't move there was because Hunter was living there and after the way we ended, I wanted as little to do with him as possible.

And while Cian shouldn't enter into my equation, somehow the notion of not seeing him again or making a life decision that immediately cuts him out of it hurts. But it's more than that. It also oddly feels... *wrong*.

But how can that be?

And where would that even leave me? We've both agreed on this being what it is and nothing more. I think we're just swept up in the whirlwind of it all. Yes, we obviously have a thing. And yes, that thing isn't just any old thing. But what happens when two people who might be right for each other meet at the wrong time? They move on and find other people who might be equally as right. Don't they?

"Come here, woman." His hands dive into my hair and his mouth captures mine. "Yer taste is my ultimate aphrodisiac. And ye can bet this sweet fuckin' arse—" He spanks me before gripping and giving my ass a good jiggle "—that's a line in my new song."

His fingers slide between my cheeks, skirting my asshole until they find my wet center. He smiles against my lips before kissing me even deeper than he was before. Tongue. Lips. Heat. Passion. His fingers plunge inside of me, and a moan flees my lungs, helplessly, recklessly diving into his mouth.

"Want you inside of me," I rasp as he picks up the pace of his fingers, his thumb now finding my clit. It's so much. The way he works my body. How his fingers move inside me. One night and this man has already made me his total worshiping whore.

He lifts me up, pressing me into the tile, and then he's there. Home base. Inside of me so deep I have to force my body to relax in order to accommodate his size. It licks the edge of pleasure and pain, especially when he starts to move, rocking up in a slow, rhythmic pattern that has me clinging that much tighter to him.

His forehead presses to mine, our eyes locked, lips layered without kissing. It's so deep like this. So intimate. The way he pushes in and up, making sure he hits me just right, driving me closer to the point of euphoric bliss. I watch his face like a woman hypnotized. The darkness of his pupils nearly eclipsing the ice blue of his eyes. The flush of lust and exertion highlighting his upper cheeks. The wet, dirty-blond hair clinging to his forehead.

His beauty is otherworldly.

A god wanted by the world seems to have found a space inside me no other will ever occupy.

"Harder," I plead, needing just a bit of roughness to drive my romantic thoughts away. And man does he know how to deliver. The hand holding my ass clenches it firmly in his fist and then suddenly I'm being pounded into the tile wall. *Slap. Slap. Slap.* Wet and loud and agonizingly perfect, he owns my body. Fucking me into oblivion. Building me higher with each thrust.

His hand slips down between our bodies, his thumb rubbing my clit as he continues to slam into me. I tremble as he fucks me.

"Ye need to come, darlin'. We're on borrowed time as it is."

I nod, already wondering if the entire house can hear what we're doing in here. If they know what we did last night. Strangely I don't care if they do. I need this man and neither heaven nor hell can keep me from him and these eight remaining promised days.

The digit on my clit starts rubbing in earnest, pressing the pad of his thumb deeper, circling harder. Within seconds I'm coming all over him, biting his shoulder so I don't scream with the fierce pleasure of it.

He follows me, grounding out words and slurring my name

in his sexy Irish brogue that seems to grow more pronounced when he's reaching his peak. And when we're both panting and smiling and kissing, he says the word. The one word I've written over and over but have never been called. Not even once.

Mine.

For now, I think. For now.

"What's up with you?" Hazel asks as we munch on pretzel bites, sitting in the atrium of the mall listening to kids scream and cry when they're forced to meet Santa in their Sunday best. "You seem... I don't know. Quiet, yes, but grumpy instead of just thoughtful as you normally are when you're quiet."

"Well, for one, we're here shopping with men. And not just any men but my brother and Hunter."

She blows out a breath, her blonde bangs puffing up in the breeze of it. "I know. It has to be Hunter who led this charge because Peter would never give up Sunday football for shopping at the mall."

I take a sip of my soda and set the cup down on the small table between us. "Why hasn't Hunter left yet?"

She gives me a dubious look. "Do you honestly need me to answer that?"

"I don't get it," I admit. "He ended it with me years ago and not in the kindest of ways either. We haven't talked or even seen each other much since. So suddenly now he's all 'I'm going to crash Christmas so I can...' What? I don't even know. He hasn't talked to me."

"That's because you won't let him."

I hitch up a shoulder. "I don't want to talk to him but more than that, I don't think it's fair to Cian."

"Speaking of, Peter might be a heavy sleeper, but I am not.

Mother, remember?" She points to her chest. "You guys were like fucking rabbits last night and even though it sounded hotter than hot, I'd be careful because if you keep up those antics, you'll wake up the whole house."

I blush, turning away from her penetrating stare and accusatory quirked eyebrow and cast my gaze out toward the fake gingerbread house and the screaming children and the flustered fake smiling Santa.

"Why do parents subject their children to this? Everyone looks miserable. Those parents are making the stupidest faces trying to get their kids to look at the camera and smile."

"It's the circle of parental torture. Our parents did it to us, so we feel we have to do the same. Not to mention, we always foolishly believe it'll turn out better than it ever does. But you're deflecting. Cian. The hot Irishman with a voice like thousand-dollar bourbon over ice and a smirk that could make even my very married panties melt. I'd ask him to sign my tits or my bra if it wasn't categorically inappropriate to do that to your sister-in-law's boyfriend and don't think your mother isn't there with me, because she is."

I turn back to her, ready to hurl my pretzel bites on the worn carpet, my nose scrunched up. "Ew. Just... ew."

A sorry-not-sorry shrug but that eyebrow hasn't dropped a notch.

"I like him," I admit.

She snorts. "Yeah, I figured since you brought him home with you and you're fucking his brains out like you'll never get the chance again. He's delicious for sure, it's just..."

"What? It's just what?"

She throws her hands up in the air. "He's just not who I thought I'd see you with. You always went for these straitlaced guys. Guys like Hunter and Peter. Cian is all bad boy hotness with tattoos and a growly alpha look to him."

"He's not like that though. I mean, he is, but he's not."

"Makes a ton of sense." She holds up her hand when I glare, unamused. "No, for real. He's not like that, but he is." Her voice escalates into the are-you-crazy territory. "He's a rock star, Viv! Like a legit, for real, in live action, top of the fucking charts, screws groupies as part of his *day job* rock star. *Soooo* not your type."

"He didn't have the happiest of childhoods," I counter, trying not to shift or gnaw on my lip.

"I know because he talked about it on *The Today Show* before his band performed on it. The fucking *Today Show* and then he was on *The Tonight Show* chatting with Jimmy Motherfucking Fallon before his band once again performed. Do you understand what I'm saying? He's famous. He's a freaking rock star. Like a no-joke one too. He posted a video of himself on IG strumming on his guitar *from your bedroom*, playing part of a new song this morning, and it already has over two million likes and hundreds of thousands of comments."

Wow, that... some stuff right there. I wonder if it's the song he was writing about me. About us. The notion of that sends a thrill through my blood.

I quickly clear my thoughts. "He's famous. I know. I don't care because I don't see that side of him. I don't check his IG or any of his social media. To me, he's different. He's Cian. A guy I seriously freaking like the hell out of. Sure, he was a total flirt at first, but that's not really who he is. He's sweet and thoughtful and soulful and..." I stop here because even though he is all these things and I do want to defend him, I'm also defending a relationship that isn't real. Hazel is right. I don't date guys like Cian. But I also can't remember a time I had feelings this quickly after meeting someone.

"You should check his IG page. You should check all his social media."

"So I can see him with other women?"

"Kind of, yeah. I'm not trying to hurt you. I just don't want you to get hurt, if you know what I'm saying."

I do. And I'm not even upset. He's not my usual type and he is famous, and this is all wrong on so many levels, but I can't help but feel the rightness of it anyway. And that's why I'm quiet today. That's why I'm grumpy. Hunter and Peter tagging along has nothing to do with it. Cian left shortly after the shower this morning and I didn't press on where he was going beyond him telling me he was running errands. It's not my business. Ugh.

I'm so tired of thinking and frankly, what's the fucking point of it anyway?

"Whatever." I stand up, tossing the empty box of pretzels and the last of my soda into a nearby trash can. "I'm going shopping." Because I still haven't gotten Cian a gift yet.

"Viv—"

I throw my hand up, stopping her. "It's fine. Go find Peter, I'm sure he's moping without you."

I start to walk away when I'm immediately intercepted by Hunter. "Hey," he says. "I was just coming to find you."

I inwardly sag. Or maybe outwardly too because he frowns a bit.

"I'm going shopping," I bite out, not meaning to sound as harsh as I do. Or maybe that's a lie.

"I'll come with you," he demands.

"I'd rather be alone."

"Don't be like that. I'll carry all your bags for you." As if to prove his point he snatches the large shopping bag that was dangling from my wrist. Now I'm trapped unless I want to body tackle him to get it back.

"Fine. But I'm shopping for Cian."

A grunt followed by another frown, but he doesn't comment as I head toward... I have no idea what to get this man. He's a rock star with his own money traveling the world on a tour bus. So whatever I get him has to be portable. But I also want it to mean something. I thought about getting him some nice whiskey or maybe a travel espresso maker because he mentioned how shitty the coffee is on the tour bus. Or maybe a cool gadget.

"Are you ever going to talk to me?"

"I wasn't planning on it," I answer him honestly, still deciding on the right store and then once I think I know where I want to start—Hazel actually gave me a cool idea—I spin around and march in the opposite direction.

"Viv, please wait." Hunter grabs my arm, stopping me in the middle of the path, causing a disruption in the force of motion that doesn't make people happy. The holiday spirit it seems, like the airport, doesn't live in the mall. He shifts us over to the side between a candle store and a Hot Topic where all the cool tweens are shopping. "Can we just have a conversation? A real one?"

Leaning against the wall, I kick my foot up into it and fold my arms across my chest. Then I look up into his brown eyes and ask the only question that requires answering. "What are you doing with me?"

A smug smirk hits his lips as he shifts to stand before me. "Trying to win you back."

I shake my head at that easy answer. "But why? It's been five years, Hunter. You made it abundantly clear to me when we broke up that you didn't want to be with me anymore. In fact, I think those were your words. 'I don't want to be together anymore, Viv. It's been three years. It's time to move on and find new people,'" I mock his voice. "So, what the fuck?"

He shifts his stance, glancing down at the ground. "I was twenty-two. You were twenty-one and had another full year of school. I was moving to New York and I... I was stupid. I was seriously stupid in thinking I'd find anyone else. That anyone else would ever be as beautiful or smart or sexy as you."

"You know nothing about the woman I am now. The girl you broke up with is not the same person I am today."

"So let me get to know the person you are today. That's all I'm asking for. A shot. A chance."

"You hurt me. You know that, right? You broke my heart and then you dug the knife deeper into my chest when you fucked those girls."

An agonized expression crosses his face. "I know. I'm so sorry. I truly am. I was... selfish and cruel. I don't even know what to say about that. It was wrong and I've regretted it every moment since that night. I knew I'd fucked up. I knew breaking up with you was a mistake. I would have tried to get you back sooner, but you were with that Harry guy."

Riiiight... that explains the three years in between, after you broke up with me and before I got together with Harry.

"Well, now I'm with Cian," I counter.

That smirk is back. "Except he's leaving for the next four months and you're not going with him. Has he even asked you to?"

No. Obviously not since I just met him. And I can't even lie and say that he has. I glance to my left, skirting his penetrating stare, not answering him. Not that it matters, the answer is glaringly obvious.

"That's what I thought. So, you're with him but that's about to end. He's a rebound guy. I get it. But after he's gone, I'll still be here trying. Why else would I voluntarily spend Christmas with your family instead of mine if I wasn't serious?"

I straighten my position, propping my hands on my hips, my face still taking in the mall around us until he clasps my chin, forcing me to look at him. I shake him off. "I don't have feelings like that for you anymore, Hunter. Five years is a long time. In fact, I've hated you longer than I loved you."

His hands cover mine over my hips, his eyes bleeding desperately into mine. "But you did love me once. You thought I was your forever. Maybe I am. Maybe we were just too young, and I was too much of a fool. Give me a second chance, Viv. Please. Move to New York. It's the best place for you and I know you know that. You've always dreamed about living there, so do it. We'll take it slow. Go on dates. Get to know each other again. I'll be so good to you, and I'll never ever betray or break your heart again. I promise."

"You say that, but looking back, I realized a long time ago that I was never right for you. I'm quirky."

"I know. You've always been quirky. I knew it then and it changes nothing about you being right for me."

"You hated that about me," I protest. "Hated that I'd randomly pull out my copy of *Persuasion* and start reading it or quote it. Hated how I'd jot down notes and lines in my notebook. Hated how lost in my head and my stories I'd get. You also hated the type of books I write. You told me writing smut was not a real profession and that if I was going to be a serious author, I should write real fiction."

He presses his hands into mine, inching in ever closer. "I didn't understand it. Again, I was stupid and ignorant. You were always different from the sorority girls, and I didn't realize that made you special and unique. And as for your writing, I was so very wrong about that too. Look how you've proved me wrong. I've followed your career and I'm so proud of you. Just as you've grown and changed, I have too. I'm not that man anymore. Please. One second chance."

"If you didn't understand me then, how can I ever expect you to understand me now?"

"Because hindsight has made me realize all that I let go of and gave up. I love that you're quirky. That you're different. That you're so fucking smart that no one can keep up with you. That your mouth constantly puts everyone in their place. I fucked up, Viv. But I never will again."

It's too much. All of this. All happening at once. Being

home with no real home of my own. Meeting Cian and getting into a fake relationship with him. Hunter giving me the full-court press.

I pull my hands out from under his and push him back. Skirting around him, I grab my bag from his wrist and start to walk away.

"You need space to think," he calls after me. "Fine. I get it. But I'm not giving up until I win you back. Cian's leaving. Guys like him are never serious about women. They use them and move on to the next. I'm real. I'm forever."

His words sting. Hitting their intended mark with deadly accuracy. Only I can't help but wish that it was the reverse. That Hunter was the one leaving, and Cian was the one staying, hoping to make me his forever.

11

CIAN

"Are you going to send me the new song, or do I have to beg for it?" Everett asks, his tone a mixture of amusement and reprimanding. I don't typically post stuff, certainly not new songs, on social media without the band being in on it. I'm not even sure why I did that in the first place other than when Vivie went downstairs for breakfast, I played it again and practically finished the entire song and was so effin' excited I couldn't contain myself.

"Already done, mate. Check the drive. I uploaded it this morning."

"Fine. But where the fuck are you? That was not your place you recorded that, and you obviously have a muse judging by the part of the song you played. You're holding out on me, Cian."

I chuckle. "It's not like that."

"But it is. So tell me who she is."

"I met an angel in the airport. I chatted her up and then we sat beside each other on the plane and once we landed, I offered to drive her home because it was late and I..." I blow out an uneven breath as I stare out the window facing the large garden in the back of Vivian's parents' home blanketed in snow. I wrote that song before I had even slept with Vivian. Now...

"And you?" he questions when I don't finish my statement.

"And I like her. I seriously fucking like her. We just hit it straight off and I didn't want dropping her off to be the end of it. But once I walked her inside her parents' home, her ex was here waiting on her and I might have put my foot in it."

"Meaning?"

"Meaning now I'm staying here through the holiday as her... fake boyfriend."

"Her what?!" he bursts out incredulously.

"Her fake boyfriend. Only it's not so fake anymore. I don't know what the hell is going on. It's only been a few days, but this woman, Everett. She's it and I'm dreading having to leave. I even like her family. Her mam is crazy but fantastic and a huge fan of ours. Her da is smart and quiet with a dry sense of humor, but I respect him. Even her wee nieces are fun."

"Shit," he murmurs, his voice low. "Cian, what are you doing getting attached to some girl you just met and her family?"

It's an easy question to ask and not such an easy one to answer. Because I don't know what I'm doing. Am I getting attached because it's Christmas and I didn't want to be alone and don't have a family of my own? Am I getting attached because I was horny and petulant and didn't want a guy like Hunter to have her since I couldn't? Or is it because her family is kind and different—like her—and treats me as one of their own without question? Is it because she's the first woman I've felt any real connection to and makes me feel special and seen for something other than my name and band? A woman who seems to see and like the odd parts of me I work so hard to hide from the rest of the world.

I think the answer is all of those things which makes it all the more complicated and confusing.

"I'm not sure I had a choice," I admit. "It hit me fast and hard and here I am."

"Are you sure she's not—"

"She didn't even know who I was when I sat down and started talking with her. She had to look me up but even once she figured it out, it hasn't seemed to change anything for her. Everett, I think she likes me for me, and I sure as hell like her. I'm an eejit. I know it. I'm leaving and she's trying to figure her own situation out."

"What does that mean?"

"She's an author. A brilliant one, but she left her old life behind and is trying to figure out a new place to live. She's staying with her family for a bit as she does that."

"So have her come with us then," he says as if it's just that easy. "You're obviously writing some seriously good shit. If she's your muse and things are going well between the two of you, have her come."

"On tour across bloody Europe and Asia for four months, sleeping on a tiny cot on a tight bus with three other blokes not even a foot away sharing one bathroom?" Our tour bus is not ideal even for us and if things continue the way they seem to be for our band, we'll have to make the big purchase and upgrade. The one from the record company is little more than a mobile dormitory. Most larger, well-established bands have their own bus designed to fit their needs.

He puffs into the phone. "Well, yeah, okay. I get it. That's pretty rough. So maybe not that. But... shit. I don't know. I see what you're saying. If there isn't a way to bring her along or keep the two of you together past this, what will you do?"

I press my hand into the glass when I see Vivie step outside, her arms wrapped around her body as she stares out at nothing, visibly thinking. The setting sun casts her body in a burnished, glowing light, making her appear even more ethereal. I want to taste the cold of the crisp air on her lips. Feel her body shiver against mine.

I've got it bad, no denying that now.

I hadn't heard her come back from her shopping trip and wonder if she even knows I've returned. I did some of my own this morning and just thinking about what I got for her has my stomach jumping. I might have gone a bit overboard with it. In fact, I know I did, but there were too many things I wanted to get her.

I turn away from the window.

"I'll try to keep her best I can for now and figure out the rest when I have to. I gotta go. I'll ring ye again soon. Merry Christmas."

"Merry Christmas, Cian, and good luck. Sounds like you need it."

"Cheers, mate. Bye."

Setting my phone down on her dresser, I go to open the door only to have it knock back in my face, hitting me square in the forehead. I stagger back a step and or a second, I'm dazed as shooting pain slices through my face. I stagger back a step.

"Ow." My hand clasps my smarting forehead, thankfully I don't feel any blood.

"Oh my gosh! Cian, I'm so sorry. I didn't know you were in here. Or at the door." Vivian's hands are on mine, gently prying my fingers away from my face. "Are you okay? You're not bleeding. Just a little red."

"Aye, I'm fine. Hardheaded as luck would have it."

"Do you want ice?"

"Nah. I hear women think wounded men and scars are sexy."

She giggles lightly and I crack my eyes open to find her smiling face right in mine. "Poor baby." She reaches up and kisses my wound. "There. That better?"

"Not sure. I think I was also hit here." I point to my cheek and her smile widens as she places a gentle kiss right on that spot. "Here too." I tap my lips and then her arms are around my neck and her sweet lips are on mine, cold from being outside.

My fingers comb through her hair, dragging her closer to me, and will I ever get enough of her? Somehow I doubt it. Only our moment doesn't last as a loud shriek pierces the air. "EWWWW! They're kissing. Gross." Fake gagging sound. "Mom, they're kissing!"

We pop apart, both of us laughing.

"Leave them alone, Willow," Hazel yells out from somewhere downstairs.

"You better be dressed," Theo barks.

"Dad, stop," Vivian calls back. "We're dressed. It was just a kiss. And besides, I'm an adult."

"Doesn't mean I like that reminder," he shoots back only to be cut off when Peter starts yelling.

"What the hell was that call? Holding? Are the refs high?"

Vivian shakes her head. "Football. That last part wasn't for us."

"I figured. Never quite understood American football, though I learned to bullshit my interest over the years."

"My dad and Peter will appreciate that when you go downstairs and watch with them while I get ready for our date. Where are we going anyway?"

"Yer mam mentioned a nice restaurant that overlooks some sort of waterfalls?"

Vivian rolls her pretty green eyes as she toys with the back of my hair at the collar of my shirt. "Figures she'd pick that place. It's the nicest in town. Also the stuffiest. I don't need anything like that. Let's go somewhere and have some fun. You mentioned dancing, I believe."

"I did find a pub not too far that has live music."

A kiss to my chin. Then both of my cheeks and finally my lips. "Let's go there. But after this morning's post, Hazel reminded me you're quite famous. Are you sure you're up for that?"

My nose glides against hers. "Were ye cross I posted that?"

She shakes her head against me. "No. Not at all. I was kind of flattered actually since I know the origin of it. But I'm worried you'll be mobbed, and we won't be able to enjoy ourselves."

I hitch up a shoulder. "I have to imagine not too many people will expect me to be out at a random pub in Connecticut."

She tilts her head, contemplating that. "Probably not, but still. Maybe you should wear a hat or something."

"Alright." Another kiss with a slip of tongue. "Get ready. I'll be waiting downstairs."

My hand slides down her back until I reach her arse where I give her a squeeze and lift her up into me so she can feel how hard I am for her and then I release her, shutting the door to her room behind me and heading downstairs to watch football with her father and brother. And likely twat Hunter too.

Sure enough, the three of them are glued to the screen in the parlor, each with a glass of beer in their hand. "Want a beer?" Theo asks without glancing my way.

"No, thank you. I'm taking Vivie out in a bit."

"Were you up there kissing my daughter?"

I can't help my smirk as I take the couch on the opposite side of Hunter since it's the only spot left. "Yes, sir. I was."

"Hmmm."

"I can't apologize for it, but I swear that's all we were doing."

"When exactly do you leave again?"

I whip over to Hunter. "Actually, mate, I think that question is more for me to ask you. Ye know, since Vivian is mine and all. I believe she's told ye she's not interested. When ye finally take the hint, let me know so I can throw ye a going away parade."

"You'll have to play your bagpipes for someone else."

A burst of laughter flees my chest. "Will I, yeah? Bagpipes are Scottish, not Irish, but I believe—and don't quote me on this—that those are played more at funerals than weddings, so I'm sure I can accommodate ye. Yer too little too late and I'm right on time."

"I wouldn't be so sure of that. You're leaving, remember?"

"No one said Vivian is moving to New York either, Hunter," her father chimes in, saving me.

"But that's the best place for her, sir," Hunter protests. "Something I'm sure you already know. Cian here is leaving and a rebound at best. Vivian deserves better than some asshole rock star who likely cheats and bangs groupies every chance he gets."

"Wrong again," I cut in. "I actually care about Vivian and would never put my own selfish needs and philandering dick before her. Ever. Honestly, yer lucky I care for her as I do otherwise I'd knock yer teeth out of yer skull for how you treated her. And if ye think I can't, read my backstory. I grew up on the poor side of Cork and then fought my way through the foster care system in the States. I ate arseholes like yerself for breakfast before I even started my day."

"Wow, we're all so impressed," he deadpans, feigning disinterest but the ruddiness of his cheeks isn't selling it. "She managed to score herself a real rebound winner. A poor Irish trash rock star with a shitty reputation. She deserves a million times better than you and you know it. Explain to me how you met Vivian again?"

"None of your damn business," she says as she enters the room. My head flies around, my eyes latching on to her, and before I know what I'm doing, I'm out of my seat, staring at the vision before me.

"Holy Christ woman, you'd make a priest sin and Jesus forgive him for the act."

She laughs. "Can I use that?"

"Use whatever you want as long as I'm included in that."

"Watch it, son."

"Right. Sorry, sir. I'm just having a wee bit of trouble dragging my tongue back in my mouth is all."

I can't take my eyes off her. She's in snug-fitting jeans and a tight, green off-the-shoulder crop top that reveals so much of her smooth, creamy, ivory skin I can hardly stand here breathing in front of her father and brother and ex-arsehole. Her red hair is half up, the bottom half curled in fat twists and her makeup is simple but sweet and shimmery.

I cross the room and my hands are around her, my lips by her ear. "God, darlin', I can't think with ye looking like this."

"Then take me to eat and spin me around a dance floor and then make me pant your name somewhere in between all that," she whispers so only I can hear.

Fuck. My cock is springing like a teenager right in front of her family. Her mam is standing in the kitchen doorway watching us with a gleam to her eyes that is unmistakable. Whether it's because of who I am or the fact that I'm clearly mad over her daughter is anyone's guess.

"I'll fulfill all yer wishes tonight."

"I'm holding you to that promise."

12

VIVIAN

The pub is loud with Sunday night drinkers, half of them crowding around the bar to watch football, the other half packed into the seats and tables. At first, I worry we won't be able to get a seat and will have to wait who knows how long, but then Cian is whispering in the hostess's ear and before I know what's happening, his hand that is holding mine is tugging me along after him.

The hostess leads us across the floor, all the way to the back where there is a small booth, half-hidden in shadows and tucked away from the majority of the rest. It's perfect. Something he tells the hostess with a big smile as he slips her a tip.

"Can I take a selfie?" she asks. "I won't tell anyone else you're here as I promised, and I'll do my best to keep the other staff and patrons away if they figure it out, but would you mind?"

"Of course not." Cian gives her his big rock star smile. The one that makes his dimples sink in impossibly deep and her sigh is audible, even over the vociferous crowd. He keeps his hat on as he slips his arm around her, and she noticeably blushes and giggles as she lifts her phone and takes the selfie.

Once that's done, he drops a light kiss to her cheek. "I'd appreciate it if ye'd hold off on posting that anywhere, at least until after we leave."

"I promise. Thank you." She moves to walk past me, only to stop and whisper in my ear. "I'm so jealous of you. He's so amazing."

And then she's gone, and I can't help but laugh lightly. He is amazing. No doubt about that. Especially when he takes my hand and helps me into the booth. Only instead of sitting on the opposite side of me, he slides in beside me, tossing his arm over my shoulder and dragging me in close to his side.

"This alright for ye?"

Is he joking?

"This is perfect for me." I grab one of the menus the hostess had placed on the table and hold it in front of us so we can both read it. "Do you drink Guinness?"

He laughs. "Because I'm Irish?"

"Well, yeah."

"Yes. I drink Guinness and yes, it is because I'm Irish. It is a bit bitter for my taste and occasionally—" He cuts off and glances around before turning back to me as if he's about to divulge a dirty secret. "—I cut it with cider, but ye have to swear you'll take that to yer grave. No self-respecting Irishman cuts his Guinness. But honestly, I prefer Belgium beer and Irish whiskey."

"I'm afraid if I start with whiskey, I'll be asleep before our dinner is served."

His ice-blue eyes sparkle as he looks at me with a smile that makes my heart hiccup in my chest. "Can't have that. What do ye normally like to drink? When I met ye, you were drinking wine. Is that yer preferred drink?"

"Sometimes. But not tonight."

His eyebrows rise questioningly just as the waitress comes over. Cian ducks his head a bit, pretending to read the menu.

It's so incredible to me, all the ways he has to hide himself so he's not recognized and subsequently mobbed. He takes it all in stride and hasn't once complained about it, but I have to imagine after a while it's taxing not being able to go anywhere without people being all over you, demanding your time.

"What can I get you two to drink?" the waitress politely asks.

"Vivie?" Cian gesticulates in my direction.

"I'll have a pumpkin spice martini with no whipped cream, please."

"Jameson neat for me. Thank you."

"Great, I'll just give you a little more time with your menus."

And then she's gone, and Cian's hands are up in my hair and his mouth is on mine, kissing me deeply. Passionately. His tongue in my mouth, flirting, dancing, coaxing mine until I'm pressed against him, pliant and content.

"I wanted to taste how sweet ye are before ye have yer drink so I can compare it to after."

And now my panties are soaked, though that's far from surprising. They've been wet since the second I saw him. Honestly, at this point, I should just stop wearing them altogether and save myself the extra laundry and clothing changes. "You keep kissing me like that and I'll forget my own name along with how to drink and eat."

He pops his hat up his head a bit so his forehead can press to mine. "'A man does not recover from such devotion of the heart to such a woman.'"

"Cian," I whisper on a shaky breath. The man is quoting Persuasion to me. Is he unaware that's the equivalent of a Vivian love potion?

"Am I coming on too strong for ye? I've always been a lead-with-the-heart sort of bloke, even when I've had to cage it so I could take one step in front of the other and make it through life."

God. This man. Can you fall for someone so soon? Is something like that even possible?

My heart is screaming, "I volunteer as tribute!" while the rest of me is attempting to remind me just how shitty heartbreak feels. Only I'm thinking heartbreak might be like childbirth when someone new and special comes along. You forget the pain of it and before you know what's happening, you're doing it again.

Or so Hazel claims since I've never experienced childbirth, only heartache.

"You're not coming on too strong. I'm just scared about what happens when our fairy bubble pops and all the magic splashes to the floor."

He's quiet for a very long moment, his eyes locked on mine from inches away. Finally he murmurs, almost begrudgingly, "Fun then?"

"Fun."

Clearly neither of us like the sound of that word.

"Or maybe we just ride this out until we can't anymore?"

"That's likely the way of it. We're the stuff of fairy tales."

"Fairy tales?"

"Aye. Once upon a time, in a land of fairy tales and beautiful maidens, there was a princess with fiery-red hair who ruled the kingdom. Her subjects worshipped her, but she always had more in her heart than simply ruling over her kingdom. She was destined for more. Then one day as she was taking a stroll outside her palace walls, she met a marauding, ruthless thief. He quickly saw her beauty and was desperate to claim it as his own. But there was a trick. A poison. A ticking clock. Like the one James Hook was so trapped by. So while the thief knew he'd never find another quite as exquisite or lovely, he also knew he was too mortal to keep such a princess as his."

"So what did this ruthless thief end up doing?" I ask, my voice uneven and shaky.

"He loved and worshipped her until the very last second he could. And even when he went on, he never forgot her. She would always be the one he'd compare every other to."

"You can't know something like that yet," I challenge.

"Ah, but I do. I knew it before I even spoke to ye."

Our drinks are delivered, cutting some of the tension and we order our food. This time we don't toast as we did the first night we met. We just raise our glasses and take a sip. Then his mouth is back on mine, getting that second taste and it's as if every pulse point and nerve ending in my body now belongs to him. He commands all my baser functions and autonomic responses.

"Cinnamon and spice, sweet, delicious, and everything nice."

"Is that what I taste like now?"

"Like fucking heaven."

"Are you moving to LA when this tour is over?"

His eyes flicker back and forth between mine in a nervous daze. "Yes. That's the plan."

"Do you like living there?"

He shifts, his hand holding his glass as he stares down at it. "Some parts of it, yeah. I like the weather and the palm trees and the ocean. I took up a bit of surfing when I first went out there and I like that too. Can't do much of that in New England and certainly not in Boston. Other things I don't like so much. But it's where Eden Dawson, our producer, lives and it's where two of my bandmates have houses, so it's how we'll go."

I hadn't thought about moving to LA. It never entered my consciousness, but now it's like I can't stop it. I won't suggest it. How insane and clingy would that be? We have no real title. We met only a few days ago. But it's as if neither one of us wants to let go. Even if it doesn't make sense to either of us.

"Do you like touring?"

"Yes. I love playing shows. The vibe and feel of them. The

pulse of the fans. The high of it. There is just something about playing music to a live audience. It's what I was born to do and it's what I'll do until my dying breath."

"I'll have to come see you sometime then."

His eyes shoot back up to mine and then his hand is on my jaw. "I'd like that. I was hoping ye'd say that even."

"What do you mean?"

He shakes his head and then our food is placed before us. He picks up a fry and pops it into his mouth, asking me about which book of mine that I've written is my favorite and just like that, all heavy topics of conversation between us are over.

He eats his burger and I eat my chicken sandwich and we drink our drinks, ordering a second round just as the band starts playing cover tunes and couples take to the floor. Cian takes my hand, dragging me out of the booth and onto the floor. His arms around my lower waist, mine circled around his neck as we sway, holding each other close. Our bodies aware time is slipping away, refusing to waste even a second together.

The song shifts to another and the moment the first beat sounds, Cian mutters out, "Bloody hell, yev got to be kidding me."

I give another listen and then I can't help the fit of giggles I fall into. "Maybe you should hop up on stage? Show them how to play and sing it the right way."

"No thanks. I'd rather be here dancing with you."

"Oh, come on. He's not half the singer you are. Will the real Cian O'Connor please stand up?"

He tickles my ribs at my teasing tone only to start singing quietly along with the band. He sings to me the entire time, his lips against mine as he does, his whiskey-tinted breath tickling my own. It's insanely sexy, the way his fingers are running along the exposed skin of my back. The way his body moves with mine. The way his eyes smolder, dark with dirty promises. The way his incredible voice serenades only me.

He's hard, pressed firmly into me and stealing my breath.

I want this man.

I want him with such savage fierceness I'm winded and ravenous.

Especially when his stubbled jaw scrapes along my cheek and his mouth hovers by my ear. "Ye asked me to make ye pant my name, if I recall."

I can't help but squirm into him. My desire multiplying when one of his hands glides up along my side, grazing my breast and nipple with his thumb.

"Now. I need you now," I tell him, my voice ragged.

The song comes to an end, another one immediately starting up and in a flash, I'm spun around, his chest to my back, his hands on my hips, pushing me away from the packed dance floor. His mouth is all over me. My neck. My shoulder. The sensitive flesh behind my ear. He can't stop kissing me and I think that's one of my favorite things about Cian. The man loves to kiss me. If he ever stops, I'll die.

All of his kisses feel like the best kisses I've ever had.

I sigh back into him, pressing myself without caring or even looking where he's taking us. There are far too many other things for me to focus on. Like the way his hand abandons my hip and presses in on my bare stomach. How it slowly starts skirting up, his fingers catching on the hem of my crop top and then inching in beneath it.

Reaching up behind me, my hands find the strands of his thick hair beneath his hat. He takes it off and drops it on my head as he walks us into a vacant event space attached to the bar. My hands slide down, latching themselves behind his neck and then both of his hands are on my breasts under my shirt. A shuddered groan pants across my ear and I shiver, my eyes closing at the delicious feel of my nipples being pulled and rolled.

"Is this still what ye want? Me to take you here?"

"Yes. And yes." I don't even care if anyone finds us. They can watch as long as they don't take pictures. I'd hate for Cian to go public in Connecticut that way. Roughly pounding a local girl with his big, thick cock in a public place. I moan at the thought.

"Ah, my woman has something specific in mind. Tell me what it is, dirty girl, and I'll give it to ye. Anything this pussy." A hand cups me over my jeans. "This heart." He squeezes my breast with his other hand. "This mind." A kiss to my temple. "Desires."

My hand slips from his neck and goes for his button and zipper, pinned between us. I squeeze his cock. Hard. "I want you to press me into a wall, any wall, I don't care, until I'm flush with it and my face has to turn to the side. Then I want you to rip my jeans down to my knees, kick my feet apart, and shove every inch of your huge cock inside me."

A slew of dirty words and curses and grunts slice the air. His face falls to my shoulder, tucking into my hair as his grip on me tightens.

"Cian?"

"I need a second, woman. Give a man a second after ye say something like that or I'll shoot in my pants like a boy."

"Does that mean you like that idea?"

He thrusts into my hand. "What does that tell ye? I'm harder than I thought humanly possible. Now walk. Show me that sweet arse I'm about to be pressed against when I flatten ye and fuck ye."

Walk? Is he kidding? I'm like two seconds from coming in *my* pants and we haven't even done anything yet. It's the buildup. It's the promise. It's the man.

Still, I manage a little—likely not as sexy as I hope—sway of my hips and wiggle of my booty until I find a wall that is smooth and not textured and then I stand in front of it, breathing hard and not daring to glance over my shoulder.

That is until he says, "Look at me. Watch as I prowl toward ye like a fucking hunter."

My face turns and I catch his eyes, first on mine with a satisfied grin to match the primal hunger of his expression, and then they drag down slowly, taking in every inch of me. The sound of the attached bar filters in, the only light seeping in from the same place, making my pulse race with excitement and anticipation.

We don't have time for the game, but he's stretching it out anyway. A master of control even as mine slips and I rub my thighs together.

"That feel good?"

"Yes."

"Do it again. Show me what yer greedy pussy needs."

Fuck. Just fuck. I grind again and he licks his lips. In a flash he's on me, pressing me into the wall exactly how I told him I wanted, squishing me until I'm flat. Then he's tearing at my jeans, ripping them open, and shoving them down my thighs. Cool air hits my ass and soaked pussy, but then he's covering those with an endless warmth. His hand presses into my pussy and he growls.

"Fucking dripping, Vivian. Yer cunt is dripping all over my hand."

He pulls his hand out and I catch him slipping his fingers into his mouth, tasting me.

"Naughty girl, ye need it, don't ye?" He smacks my ass. Hard. I jerk into the wall, rubbing against it like a mindless fool. He smacks me again with the same wet hand and then I hear his zipper.

I whimper, my eyes closing as he kicks my feet apart, widening my stance.

Only nothing happens.

"Cian. Please."

His fingers are back, rubbing my clit as the blunt head of his cock presses in against my entrance. I moan loudly only to have his mouth cover mine. "Ye moan like that and yer going to get us caught. Is that what ye want?"

Is it? I don't know. Kinda. Sorta. Maybe. Possibly. It's always so hot in my books, but in reality?

I push back, seeking more of him only to have him slam inside of me with all his might. His lips stifle my scream and then he's pounding into me. Giving me everything I wanted and asked for. Fulfilling my dirty, public, slightly forceful and rough fantasy.

"Fucking Christ, yer tight like this." One hand wraps around my neck without restricting my breathing, the other is on my hip in a bruising grip. "Ye want my cum?"

"Yes."

"Yer going to have to coat me in yours first."

Jesus hell. No one has ever fucked me like this. Ever given me exactly what I want. I'm not into crazy kink, but I'm not vanilla either, and if I needed more confirmation that I've been with the wrong men all this time, the way Cian is fucking me now is all the proof I need.

His hips piston into mine, the teeth of his zipper scraping at the globes of my ass. His hand on my neck holds my face against his shoulder and for a second, I'm annoyed that he's changing up the fantasy, but then I realize with the pounding slamming of my body into the wall, he's protecting my skin.

Even with the barbaric way he's taking my body, he's still looking out for me. Making sure I'm okay and taken care of.

A bolt of pleasure shoots through me like lightning through the sky, burning a path so hot and brilliant it sets every cell I have on fire. Grunts and groans and curses mixed with the filthiest words spill from his lips into my ear. His cock fills me up with rapid, short, tight thrusts. This angle doesn't allow for slow pulls or long, languid drags.

It's powerful and wet and so good my eyes roll back in my

head when he gives my neck just the smallest of squeezes. *God yes*, I think. I'm getting so close, crackles of light flirt and play behind my eyes. His finger finds my clit, rolling it only to pinch it, and I detonate. Exploding all over him, feeling myself gush as I'm propelled vigorously into the wall. Something about that makes me come harder, clench tighter, and then Cian is there too.

Hands gripping me, body pressed against mine, he comes with his hot breath against my ear. He stills, shuddering and shaking, hissing and rumbling until he's as spent as I am. With a sharp breath, he releases my neck, replacing the contact with his lips. Kissing and licking where he was squeezing.

He mumbles something I can't make out against my skin as his arms wrap themselves around me and for a moment, he holds me like this. Against his body. His heart pounding into me. That is until a sound not too far from us has him jerking, frantically tucking himself back in his pants and yanking my jeans back up my hips.

He takes my hand, snatching a cloth napkin off a nearby table and handing it to me as he directs us toward the bathrooms at such a quick pace, my shaky, heeled feet can hardly keep up. We reach the ladies' room, and then he's knocking before opening the door for me.

"Vivian?"

In a daze, I turn to look at him, his eyes tender and bewildered in awe. His mouth is on mine, his hands up in my hair as he kisses me. With a serious expression, he pulls back, cups my jaw, and then leaves me to go into the ladies' room as he heads for the men's next door.

I shut and lock the door behind me and blow out a heavy breath, only to laugh when I catch sight of my reflection in the mirror. "Best sex of your life with the man of your dreams. What could go wrong?"

13

CIAN

Vivian and I spent the rest of the evening driving around. She showed me where she went to school and where she used to play softball and take gymnastics and even where she got her first kiss. That's where we are now, the car in park, music playing through the sound system, and our mouths attacking each other like a couple of teenagers before curfew.

The woman has me twisted up from the inside out.

What we just did in the bar... *Hell*. I'm insatiable. I'm wrecked and ruined.

I want her the way I've never wanted another woman.

I care about her the way I've never cared about another woman.

I'm in love with her the way—*wait*. What?

No. That's rubbish. I've never been in love before and it's far too soon. A person can't fall in love in a matter of days. That's certainly not what this is. But now that the thought has been implanted, it won't quit or die or be stuffed back into the spot in my brain it came from.

The notion of it stuns me so dramatically that I'm gasping

for air against her mouth, and it has nothing to do with how incredible her kisses are. Suddenly I'm overtaken with disorienting, soul-quaking dizziness that slams into me like a truck. I can't think of anything else other than what feels like a staggering truth.

I love Vivian Scott.

I might have even loved her the moment I saw her. Romeo finding his Juliet. Perseus to his Andromeda.

And I'm going to leave her in less than a week for tour. A tour that takes me across the world from her. Panic swims through me causing me to attack her mouth with a fresh burst of urgency.

"Cian—"

Only that's as far as she gets because there is a knock on my driver's side window that is completely fogged over with steam. Startled, we jump apart, certainly feeling more like teenagers now that we've been caught by... the police. Just bloody grand. Of course we get caught when we're acting the maggot in a place we shouldn't be.

I roll down the window to the blinding light of a torch in my face and the frigid, icy bite of December. "Can I see your license, registration, and proof of insurance?"

"Em. Sure, officer."

I toss Vivie a side-eye and then snake out my wallet as she goes into the glove box and retrieves the rental agreement information since that's all I have at present. She hands it to me, and I do the same to him.

He takes everything. "Did you know you're trespassing in a public park that closes at sundown?"

I didn't care enough to give it thought. "I wasn't aware of that, no."

"You're a little old to be making out in the car, aren't you?"

Christ. Is he for real?

I want to smart off so badly, but wisely I just keep my mouth shut. Vivian is hunched over in my direction, squinting up at the cop. I'm about to throw her a look that says stop glaring at the man before he arrests us or performs a cavity search on us both when she says, "Jacob? Is that you?"

The cop finally lowers his light, ducking his head so he can see inside. He stares at Vivian for a moment and then a smile spears his lips. "Vivian? Wow, I haven't seen you since graduation."

"Same. How are you? You're a police officer now?"

"Yes." His forearms drop to the windowsill as he leans his head practically inside the car, ignoring me completely now. "Joined the force after I graduated UCONN. How have you been? I heard you're a big-time author now."

Vivian laughs and just what the hell is going on here?

"No, well, I am an author, but I'd hardly call myself big time."

Jacob, the police officer, shakes his head. "That's not the way I heard it. You're all Melinda has been talking about. She reads all your books."

Vivian gasps. "Melinda Reeves? Oh my gosh, I haven't seen her in forever."

He holds up his left hand, showcasing a gold wedding band, and Vivian gasps again.

"You're married to her?! That's amazing. Congratulations. Please, you'll have to tell her I say hello."

"For sure. But what the hell are you doing in this park other than the obvious? You know better. We got caught doing the same thing here forever ago." Then he laughs. "Remember that? The police made us go home and tell our parents what we were doing."

Vivian laughs too and ha bloody ha, it's all just so funny. The idea of Vivian making out with this guy, the same way she just was with me, has my blood running cold and a frown tugging down the corners of my mouth. I want to break his nose just so I can knock the smile from his face. Even if she is distracting him from hopefully giving us a ticket. Or heaven forbid making me return to her house and tell her father all that we've done tonight.

"I know. Wow, that was so embarrassing. My dad wouldn't let you in the house again until after we broke up."

More laughter. "Right. I remember that. Good times."

Good times? Is he for real?

"I know we shouldn't be here, but I was showing Cian some of the old stomping ground and well, you know." Vivian shrugs sheepishly with a hint of a blush on her cheeks.

"Fine. I'll let you go with a warning, but please promise to keep it behind closed doors and not venture into public parks after dark."

The officer hands me back my license and the paperwork.

"We will," she exclaims solemnly. "I promise. Oh, we should get together. The four of us, if there's time before Cian has to leave. I'd love to catch up more with you and see Melinda."

"Yes! She'd love that. Does she have your number?"

Vivian shakes her head, and I cannot believe this is happening right now. "No. I doubt it. Here." She fishes in her purse, pulling out her notebook and scribbling her number down before handing it to her old chum. "Have her call or text and we'll figure something out."

"Sounds good. Have a good night."

Jacob gives us a wave and then he's marching back to his cruiser that's just on the other side of my door. He gets in and I roll up the window before turning on her. "Ye made out with that man here?"

She gives me a look. "Good thing I did or we'd either be arrested or sitting with a fat ticket."

"I wanted to kill the man, married, a cop, or not."

She rolls her eyes at me. "Don't be dramatic. We hardly dated for long. Just a few months."

"A few months!"

She's laughing at me now with her eyes as she chews on her swollen lip. "I was sixteen."

"That doesn't help."

"I'm sleeping with you now."

"Not enough. Give me something else."

"You're the best sex I've ever had."

"Marginally better. Tell me ye didn't fuck him."

"I didn't fuck him. We only got to third base."

"Jesus Christ, Vivie, yer going to make me postal." I run my hands through my hair but she's there, catching them and bringing them to her lips. Kissing my knuckles one by one.

"How about you take me home instead and I can spend the rest of the night showing you with my mouth and body how much I want you and no one else."

I relax. A little. Not a lot because I'm still all fired up from the love bomb my brain and heart dropped on me. "Nice one. But I think it's safe to say I'm going to ruin yer body tonight so ye never even think about another bloke again other than me."

Except as the words leave my mouth, I inwardly wince. Because there is no way I can keep her. And my time is nearly running out.

LIFE IS what happens when you allow yourself to let go and experience it. Fear is what holds you back and gives you regrets. That's what I had always told myself. That I'd had enough fear as a child and that as an adult, I wouldn't let it rule me again. And while the first part of my mantra is how I got here and why I'm with Vivian, the second part, the one I swore I'd never battle again, is gripping me by the throat and strangling me.

She's fast asleep on top of me. Not in her top bunk but tucked on me in this tiny twin-size bed. We laughed about it.

First, we had sex on it, and then when she climbed on top of me because I wouldn't let her go, she said, "I guess as long as I'm on top, then I'm not breaking the rules."

We're breaking the rules. We're breaking all kinds of rules, no matter what she says.

But now it's somewhere near morning I think and I'm awake. Unmoving, holding her against me, but awake, nonetheless. It's all because of that damn fear.

I'm afraid of loving this woman.

I'm afraid it's already too late.

I'm afraid of what this love will do to me.

I'm afraid she simply doesn't feel the same way back because loving her like this so soon is crazy and impetuous and nonsensical and none of those things describe who Vivian is as a person. She likes her plans. She sticks to the rules.

I'm also jealous of Hunter again.

Not because she'll necessarily end up with him, but the option is there. The option for a million other lovers is there for her. I've never had a possessive or jealous moment when it came to a woman. Not once. Until Vivian.

I don't know what I can ask of her or even if I have the right. We agreed on the here and now. On fake. On a break in reality that we both know we'll have to return to and that when we do, we'll have to do it without the other.

It's starting to feel as though something vital is slipping away from me—time, yes, but something else with it too. Happiness. A happiness that feels brand new and sparkly and precious and terrifyingly fleeting. And for the first time ever, I don't love the demands of my job.

I'm trying to hold it all off. Shove it away. All this fear and loneliness and love and anger. I force myself to remember that my time with her *is* fleeting and that wasting it on those useless emotions will only cause more hurt in the end.

I try reinvigorating the fun and naughty of what we're doing in my head.

Today is Christmas Eve so that's not helping my shite mood either.

"I feel you burning like a lump of coal Santa dropped in your stocking. Not getting your Christmas wish?"

I smirk. And then I tickle her side boob because it's sexy. "Yer my Christmas wish." And fuck. Why the hell did I have to go there? Just like that? Like my brain has no filter. "Just don't love Christmas so much anymore, ye know?"

"Do you know my favorite thing about Christmas Eve?" She pops her face up, planting her elbow into the mattress beside my head so she can gaze down at me.

"No. What?" Christ, I could stare into her mint-green eyes and glowing face forever and never grow tired.

"No. What?"

"Making cookies for Santa that I get to eat that night after the girls have gone to sleep since obviously Santa doesn't slide down my chimney."

"He better not slide down or up any chimney of yours."

She giggles when I tickle her other side, rolling us so she's now on bottom and I'm on top, her father be damned.

"You're a bit of a caveman."

"So it seems, but only with you. C'mere, darlin'." I grasp the back of her head and dip my face down to hers so I can kiss her crazy before we're forced to get up and face a household of her family.

And just when things start to get good, a pounding comes from her door. "Penny and Willow are already tossing chocolate chips and snickerdoodle batter around the kitchen. Where the hell are you?"

She smiles into me. "Cookie baking time. Maybe I'll save some dough and you can lick it off me later."

"Worth the risk of salmonella."

A deep, searing, over far too quickly kiss. “Stop moping. Today’s going to be so much fun.”

She isn’t wrong either.

We bake cookies, getting into a small dough fight that has her mother yelling at us. Then we mix six different martinis and sample four different wines because, apparently, we have to find the perfect before-meal cocktail and the just-right-with-dinner accompaniment.

All it does is leave us a bit drunk. To the point where we burn two batches of cookies and I get talked into singing and playing Christmas carols with the girls. I don’t even care when Willow snaps a string on my guitar. Darla asks me a million questions about an Irish Christmas, which frankly, I don’t know the answers to.

She tells me at the end of it all that she did some Google research and hopes I’ll feel comfortable and at home tomorrow since I can’t be with my mam. Maybe it’s the copious amounts of alcohol and sugar, but I hug the woman fiercely. And I might get a wee bit choked up. Because no one has given a rat's arse about my comfort or tried to make me feel at home since my mam and even then, it was all we could do to survive from day to day.

Comfort and at home aren’t things I’m all that familiar with but I am starting to realize the necessity behind them.

Dinner is served with more alcohol followed by more sugar and maybe it’s all the Christmas cheer, but I even manage to feel bad for Hunter who is staring longingly at Vivian like she’s his missing piece. I don’t even kick his arse when he attempts to shift her under the mistletoe that’s hanging between the dining room and the parlor.

It seems the alcohol and sugar and general merriment are causing me to not care about a lot of things.

Including my missed phone calls.

14

VIVIAN

"Merry Christmas," everyone yells as we walk downstairs bright and early. Penny and Willow pounded on our door at six, their squeals and laughter reverberating through the house and after that, no one was getting any sleep.

Cian's adorably rumpled with his hair half standing on his head and two days' worth of scruff on his rugged jaw. We're both still in our pajamas though mine says "What up Grinches." The girls are already sitting around the tree, chomping at the bit, staring at the myriad of colorfully wrapped gifts. The plate of cookies we left out for Santa is sitting empty, same with the glass of milk.

My father is in his chair in a prime spot to play Santa as he always does, and my mother is demanding we give her two minutes so she can get the breakfast casserole into the oven.

"Merry Christmas, Viv," Peter murmurs to me, pulling me in for a hug. "Fifty says you return half the things you get."

I laugh, shoving him back. "And fifty says you donate half the things you get."

"I'm not taking that bet and you're not either since we both know how this always ends."

"In returns and donations," I agree.

Hazel rolls her tired eyes at us while yawning. "You're both the worst to shop for."

"Are not," we say in unison. "We're just particular," Peter finishes.

"Vivian never returned the presents I bought for her," Hunter says, coming in beside me and practically pushing Peter out of the way so he can give me a hug.

"That's because you always got me things I couldn't return, like dinners and mini vacations."

He shrugs. "Can't help it if I was crafty enough to know better than to buy you something tangible. Merry Christmas, Viv." A kiss to my forehead that has Cian grunting.

"Daddy!" Willow cries out. "Presents! I want to see if Santa got my letter about the Poopsie Surprise."

"He didn't," Peter replies.

"Poopsie Surprise?" I question.

Hazel groans. "Don't ask. It's this crazy unicorn thing that poops out slime. It's freaking disgusting."

I hold up my hands. "I don't want to know."

"Come sit down." My father waves us over. "Darla, I'm starting."

"I'm there in two seconds," she yells back from the kitchen and all of us crowd in, sitting around the tree. The fire is going in the fireplace, classic Christmas music is crooning softly in the background, and outside flurries are falling from the gray sky.

It's absolutely perfect. Everything Christmas should be.

Cian tucks in behind me on the ground, leaning his back against the sofa and dragging me into his chest. "Merry Christmas, Vivie Girl."

I press into him, turning so I can steal a quick kiss on his lips. "Merry Christmas." His fingers brush a few strands of hair back from my face. And for a moment, everything else fades but him. The way he feels surrounding me. The way his eyes stare into mine. I'm so lost in him. Yesterday was one of the best days I ever remember having and all of that had to do with him. Sharing Christmas with my family with him.

Getting to know him the way I have.

The sex and the fire and the passion and the love. There, I said it, because hell if it's not there too. I was with Harry for two years and I would have told anyone who asked that I loved him but being with Cian is soul awakening. He has me rethinking everything and it hasn't even been a damn week yet.

I don't want him to go. And I can't ask him to stay.

"Alright, alright," my father calls out, snapping my attention away from Cian. "Willow and Penny, you start. Pick up a present and hand it to me so I can start passing them out."

The girls dive into the mass with gusto. "This one says my name!" Penny squeals in delight before she starts tearing at the paper. "Poopsie! I got Poopsie!"

"No fair. I want Poopsie."

My mother rushes in, picking up another similarly wrapped gift. "Willow, baby, I think this one is for you."

"Mom, I can't believe you."

"What?" She waves Peter's whining complaint away. "It's from Santa. Oh, and I think this one is for Cian. Here." She tosses a flat green wrapped gift at him. He catches it with a bemused look that makes my mother smile. "You didn't think we wouldn't get you anything, did you?"

"Em. Well. I…" He clears his throat. "Thank you. I wasn't expecting anything."

He carefully starts removing the paper and I laugh. "Oh my god. Please tell me you're not one of those people." I shift, ripping the paper a little.

He grins. "Just savoring the moment, darlin'." But then he

loses his patience and rips it the rest of the way, revealing a black T-shirt. He unfolds it and bursts out laughing.

"What? What is it?"

He spins it around so all of us can see. On the top, written in red scroll it says, Chest. On the bottom of the shirt, toward the hem, it says, Nuts in the same red font.

"Get it," my mom prompts. "Chestnuts. Chest. Nuts."

I can't help the incredulous laughter that flies out of my mouth. "Mom! I can't believe you got him that."

"It's funny." She takes a sip of her coffee, sitting on the arm of my father's chair. "There's more."

He ruts back through the now ruined paper and pulls out a Connecticut baseball hat. "To help you keep that low profile and so you always remember your time here, though we're hoping you'll be back sooner than not."

"I love it. Thank you so much." He shakes his head and climbs up to his feet, crossing the room and hugging my mother like she's his lifeline. He hugs my father too. "I'm so grateful to ye fer having me in yer home and making me feel part of yer family like this. I can't tell ye what it means to me."

After that, everything turns into bedlam. Toys and presents strewn about. Paper and bows flying every which way. Coffee is finally doled out, all the adults grateful for the caffeine jolt. Peter gives Hazel a gift card to her favorite furniture shop in Brooklyn, which seems to make her very happy. My father gives my mother tickets to a Broadway show and a night at a nice hotel in New York. Hunter gives everyone something different and expensive.

Cian got the girls American Girl dolls that they went nuts over. He gave my mom a wine of the month club membership and a signed band T-shirt as well as a full access badge. He promises her any time she wants to come see a show, she's got front-row tickets. He gives Hazel something similar. My dad gets crystal brandy glasses as well as an expensive bottle of Remy Martin cognac.

"Here. I got this for you, Viv." Hunter hands me a small box that I hesitantly open, all the while feeling Cian's eyes and scowl on me. It's a solid gold key chain engraved with the words, someone in New York loves you and a key hanging off the loop. "It's a key to my place in the city," he says. "I'm hoping you'll use it when you're ready and the time is right."

"Hunter—"

I don't know what to say. For once I'm at a loss for words. It seems... wholly inappropriate for too many reasons to count. And weirdly sweet in some strange way. Obviously I can't accept it and frankly, I don't want it, but can I just give it back to him?

"That's a nice shot yer taking there," Cian says, his voice cooler than the icy frost of his eyes.

"Just making my wishes and desires abundantly clear," Hunter replies evenly. "You know, because you're leaving."

"Doesn't mean she's going to be yours again, mate."

"Doesn't mean she won't be either. Don't think for a second I don't know what game you're playing. How long have you been dating her again?" Hunter questions, squinting his eyes as if he knows something.

My heart rate picks up a beat as Cian answers, "About six weeks."

"Interesting."

"How's that now?" Cian parries and I know everyone is watching us, listening with the exception of Willow and Penny who are working out Barbie negotiations.

"Well," Hunter continues, his voice sharper than a blade. "You see, since you posted that part of your song the other morning and all the women of the house made us listen to it, I got curious and did a bit more digging."

Oh fuck. Cian shifts, dragging me closer to his side. "Good for you. So happy you've learned how to navigate social media."

"What's this about?" Peter asks, taking a sip of his coffee and dragging his eyes away from his daughters.

"I just got curious about our Irish friend is all," Hunter explains. "So I searched your name since most of the images you have on your profile are about your band. Do you want to tell everyone what I found?"

Cian snorts out a halfhearted attempt at a laugh. "Hunter, how about you stop being a total slag and just tell me what you think you found on there."

"This."

He tosses his phone over to me and it lands on my lap. I pick it up and see an Instagram picture of Cian in a club in Miami with two women on either side of him though he's hardly paying them any attention as it looks like he's talking to someone who isn't in the image. It was posted on one of the women's Instagram profiles.

"This is a publicity shot at a club my band was asked to attend," Cian says after glancing at the image. "Those are models and influencers hired by the club. Not dates."

"And you mean to tell us you didn't screw either of them or any of the other women there?"

"Cian, you don't have to—"

"No. it's fine," he tells me with a smile that doesn't touch his eyes. He releases a sigh, running a hand through his hair. I sit up straighter and turn my body in his direction, letting him feel the full force of me. I know where this is headed. Clearly Hunter knows the truth. I hadn't thought much about our fake relationship in the last few days because it stopped feeling fake pretty damn quickly.

Cian didn't know me when this picture was taken of course, but that doesn't change what they'll see if they keep searching.

Hell, even I found it without having to look too hard. Cian traveling and touring. Women all around him.

"No. I didn't sleep with any of those women that night," he says. "And that's the God's honest truth."

He told me he hadn't slept with anyone before me in over a month and I believe him. He's never lied to me. Not once about anything and he'd have no reason to lie about that.

"But you weren't with Vivian there, right?" That's Peter and just fabulous that he's now getting in on this.

"Vivian was not with me in Miami."

"Right," Hunter maintains as if Cian just proved his point. "Miami wasn't your only stop either. In fact, according to your touring schedule, which I found on your website, you weren't in DC until last week. How could the two of you have met and been together if you were traveling and she was in DC? And before you go and feed us some bullshit about her traveling to see you, we know she didn't. She also didn't mention a thing about you until you were here in this house."

"That's because they weren't actually together until they were here in this house."

My head snaps over in my dad's direction, my eyes wide and unblinking, my heart stopping altogether.

"What?" Peter and Hunter exclaim in unison.

My dad takes a slow sip of his coffee, his eyes trained on the fire, keeping us all in suspense. "The night Vivian came home, she introduced Cian as her friend and asked if he could spend the night on the couch in my study since it was so late, and he had given her a ride home from the airport. Then suddenly Hunter was standing there, and Vivian was upset about that. She felt ambushed." My father turns back to us, his eyes on Cian. "You saw how upset she was and then you claimed her as your girlfriend. It honestly didn't take much to put the pieces together."

"You knew?" I'm flabbergasted.

"Of course I knew. I'm your father. We talk twice a week at least. If you were dating Cian before that, I would have heard about him."

"But..." I trail off, unsure what to say or do next. He knew. All this time he knew Cian and I weren't together. And yet he let him stay. In my room no less.

"Why did ye let me stay then?" Cian asks, voicing my unspoken question.

My father sets his mug down. "Because I saw the way you were looking at her and then I watched as you stood up for her. I assumed you'd be gone by the morning as she said, and I couldn't exactly kick you out in the middle of the night after you drove my daughter home. But then Vivian told you she wanted you to stay."

"Because I did," I cut in, my eyes on Cian.

"So you're not together?" Hunter is on his feet now. "I knew it. I fucking knew it."

"Well, I wouldn't be so sure about that anymore," Hazel chimes in. "They're obviously together now, they just weren't then."

"Yes," I say. "I'm sorry we lied."

"I knew he was a loser, but a liar too."

Cian stands once more, ignoring Hunter and walking over to my parents. "I'm sorry. I didn't mean to mislead ye. I just..." He swallows and reaches his hand out to shake my dad's. "I care about your daughter a great deal, sir, and though I'm not sure what will happen when I leave in a few days, I'd like your permission to stay and continue to date her for as long as she'll allow it."

"The fuck?!" Hunter is pacing now. "You lied to us about dating her and now you're saying this shit? Get out!"

"Wait." Peter is on his feet now too. "So, you weren't together but now you are?"

"Oh, they're dating alright," my mom says with a gleam to

her eyes. "Haven't you seen them together? They're like we were, Theo, when we were that age. Your father couldn't keep his hands off me, same as Cian is with Vivian." She sighs dreamily. "Those were some good days. I need to go check on the casserole, but Cian, you're welcome to stay here as long as you'd like."

"Cian, I believe that you're sincere in liking my daughter," my dad says, not addressing any of that. I turn back to him. "The only thing I ask is total and complete honesty with us as well as Vivian from here on out. If you're good to her, you can stay and date her. If you're not, well, I'll let both Peter and Hunter have at you and when they're done, I'll tie you up and leave you in the snow to freeze to death." He shakes Cian's still outstretched hand. "Am I understood?"

"Absolutely, sir. No more lying. I promise."

"No. Stop. This is insane. They lied. How on earth are you okay with him and not me?" Hunter is pouting now. "I'm here. I gave her a key to my home. To my heart. I'm not leaving to travel the world and I won't break her heart."

"Again, you mean?" my dad points out. "I never liked you because you were always a wormy bastard who put himself above everyone else. You never treated Vivian with any respect for who she is and certainly never the way she deserved to be treated. Then you broke her heart in a cruel and callous way."

Hunter shakes his head, his hands on his hips. "I apologized to Vivian the other day for all of that. I was young and stupid, but that's not who I am anymore."

"Hunter, that apology is five years too damn late. More importantly, it shouldn't have happened like that in the first place. If you ever cared or respected my daughter as you ought to have, then you would have been a better man to her."

"I feel like I'm watching *Days of Our Lives,* only no one is in a coma, and no one is about to be blackmailed," Hazel hisses to me. “Incidentally, you should have told me. Fake relationships are my favorite trope.”

I snicker. “Totally,” I agree conspiratorially. “Only, this isn’t a romance novel.”

“But you should write it into one. Make Cian an athlete instead of a rock star if you have to for your brand.”

Hunter, Cian, Peter, and my dad are still going back and forth, things growing more heated by the second.

“Look,” I cry out so I can be heard above everyone else. “Just stop. I am a grown woman, and I can make the decision on who I’m dating and who I’m not. Hunter, I already told you how things are. While I appreciate the gift you gave me, five years is a long time and honestly, I’m not interested in repeating my past mistakes. I’m sorry, but it’s not going to happen.” I turn on Cian now. “And you.” I shove a stern finger into his hard chest. “If you want to date me for real, how about asking *me* instead of my father about that?”

He fights his dimpled grin and fails miserably. “I believe I already did that, and nothing has been fake for me. Not once with ye. I was simply being respectful to yer da after I was anything but by lying. But, if ye need something else from me...” He trails off and then moves around the tree to pick up a large, wrapped box. “Here. I got you this.”

15

CIAN

Vivian's eyes search mine and my skin suddenly feels feverish as a cold sweat breaks out on the back of my neck. I likely went too far with this. Practicality states that my feelings for Vivian are much stronger than hers are for me. Not just that, I haven't seen any indication to speak otherwise. Yes, she likes me, but what I'm giving her clearly shows my feelings run deeper than that.

Hunter gave her a damn gold key ring and she rejected it and him.

So to say I'm nervous is an understatement.

Speaking of Hunter, I don't see him anywhere. Hopefully he's gone to pack and leave.

But I can't focus on him right now. Not when Vivian is opening the paper and then the lid of the box. With curiosity lighting her features she sifts through the paper and removes the second small box, setting it to the side and focusing on the large thing beneath it only to gasp when she realizes what it is.

I sit beside her on the sofa, angled in so our knees are touching. "I got one fer myself too. Figured it was easier than always trying to keep track of where I left off and having to find a pen."

"It's a note taker."

"Aye. You use the stylus if ye want like a pen and it transcribes your writing down into notes. You can create tabs and folders and organize yer stuff however ye want it. It also does audio notes, so you can say something if ye don't want to write it down."

"It saves everything to the cloud and drives if I want. I can even email them to myself."

I nod. "That way ye won't lose everything if ye ever lost yer notebook and ye don't have to transcribe things over and over."

"It's incredible. I had no idea something like this was out there. Thank you." She turns to me with a smile that makes my furiously beating heart jump only to have my chest clench painfully tight when she moves onto the small box.

"If ye don't like it or it's too much, I can return it," I tell her, remembering the teasing earlier between her and Peter.

"Don't say that because not only will I not return anything you get me, but you can't return what I got you."

She throws me a quick wink and then she's back to the box, slowly opening the top.

"Jesus. Cian." With delicate, slightly tremulous fingers, she reaches in and pulls out the platinum charm bracelet.

"Each of these is a piece of us. I've told ye I'm not sure what happens to us when I go, but no matter what, I want you to know how much ye mean to me and how much I—" *Not the right time for those words, Cian!* "—have loved being here with you."

I take it from her hand and undo the clasp, securing it around her dainty wrist. I finger the charms one by one. "A guitar, a book, an airplane, a whiskey glass, a Christmas tree, a music note, a snowflake, a car, and... a Celtic love knot."

"Is that..."

"An emerald in the center. The color of yer eyes."

"It's beautiful," she rasps, twisting her wrist this way and that so she can take it in. Tears roll down her face and I smear a couple of them away with my thumbs. "I love everything about it, and I hate all that it will eventually represent."

"I know, darlin'. Me too." I lean in and kiss her cheek, catching a tear with my lips.

"Well." She emits a shaky laugh, wiping her face. "I got you something that I hope you'll love and hate equally as much."

"Fan-bloody-tastic. Bring it on."

She rises to move to the tree only to stop short and look around the room. We're alone in here, neither of us having realized the others left us to have a moment together. It makes this both better and worse. Exchanging gifts like this feels like goodbye. It feels like the end.

It's tearing me up inside.

Vivian kneels in front of me with two things. One is a bag, the other is a box.

"I didn't know what to get you. You're not an easy man to shop for."

"You should try shopping fer you."

She laughs, her cheek falling to my thigh, resting there. "I love what you got me."

And I love you. I run my fingers through her hair, the words I've nearly said a dozen times to her in the two days since I realized them singeing the tip of my tongue.

"Open them. Start with the box first."

Sitting back on her heels, she watches me with an uneasy yet hopeful expression. I do as I'm told, unwrapping the large box first and grinning like a fool when I see it. "An espresso maker."

"A travel one. It got good reviews. It's also pretty and modern. It was in the MOMA if you can believe it."

"Darlin', this is absolutely perfect. You have no idea how shite the coffee is on the road nor how badly we need it."

"Well, now all of you can have fancy coffee."

"Thank you."

I lean in and press my lips to hers.

"There's more."

Pulling the red tissue paper out of the green bag, I reach in, finding what feels like a small wooden block. Vivian is chewing teeth marks into her lip as she watches me take it out and flip it over. But the moment I see what it is, my eyes instantly glass over. "Vivian," I whisper, my voice catching.

"I found that picture on your Instagram the night we met before I got on the plane," she says. "I hope you don't mind. I wasn't sure if you carried any pictures around with you while you tour, and you had mentioned how you're an Oscar Wilde fan."

"It's... ah, bloody hell, I'm speechless." I can't remove my eyes from it. "Thank you. Thank you so much."

I wipe at my face, dumbstruck. Overwhelmed. So fucking in love with this caring, compassionate, lovely fucking woman. It's a picture of me with my mam on my sixteenth birthday, two months before she died. It's also the only picture I ever had of the two of us and I put it on my Instagram on the anniversary of her death one year. Not for attention—hell, I don't even have a caption beneath it—but so it'd be there with me no matter where I went.

I could always access it.

Vivian had a copy of it made and somehow placed on this small wood box. The Oscar Wilde inscription curved along the outside of the image. *"You don't love someone for their looks, or their clothes or their fancy car, but because they sing a song only you can hear."*

I set it down in my lap and cup her face with both hands, staring into her eyes. "Vivian, from the moment I saw ye sitting in that bar, I knew you were someone I had to talk to. Had to meet. But in these last several days with ye, you've become something so much more to me." I lick my lips, my heart pounding wildly in my chest. "Vivie... I know this might seem crazy, but I have to tell ye anyway. I—"

"Cian?" Hazel's voice rings out from the stairs, cutting me off. With a growl, my eyes snap over to her. "I'm so sorry to interrupt, but your phone has been ringing nonstop. I figured it might be something important."

And just as she says the words, my phone in her hand starts ringing.

"Shite." I leap up off the couch and race over to her, worried there's something wrong with one of my bandmates. No one calls repeatedly on a holiday if there isn't something wrong.

And sure enough, it's my manager.

I swipe my finger across the screen. "Terry?"

"Cian, I'm so sorry to bother you while you're on holiday, man."

"That's all right," I say, racing up the stairs and into Vivian's room for some privacy. "What is it?"

"It's your dad."

"My dad?" I parrot, my steps faltering.

"Yes. I've been trying to reach you since yesterday. A lawyer in Ireland contacted me since he was unable to locate you directly. I did some checking before calling you and it's legit. Your father, I'm so sorry to tell you, passed away four days ago."

I tumble down onto the bottom bunk, my thighs parted as I stare aimlessly about Vivian's room. "I haven't seen or heard from my father in donkey's years. Well over a decade."

"I know, man. I know. But you're his only living relative and the heir to his estate."

I practically throw up in my mouth, only it comes out as a sardonic scarf. "What fucking estate?"

"Evidently he won the lottery several years back."

A humorless chuckle flees my lungs. "He won the lottery? Are ye kidding me here?"

"No. The attorneys wouldn't give me any further information than that, but from the sound of it, it's a lot of money you're about to inherit."

I scrub a hand over my face. "How did he die?"

"Heart attack. His housekeeper found him."

"Shitehawk motherfucker that he was didn't deserve something that easy." No, he should have suffered the way mam did. A hundred times worse for how he treated her. How he treated us.

"Cian, the attorneys asked you to come to Ireland to settle his affairs."

"I'm coming to Ireland on the thirtieth."

"Right," he says, but there is no agreement in it. "You're going there for less than forty-eight hours before moving on to the rest of the tour. I know you hated your dad. I know you have very solid reasons for that. But this has to be taken care of before the tour starts."

I fall back on the bed, staring up at the slats overhead. "I don't want to leave early. Especially not for him."

"Except it has to be done. That's how these things go. Trust me on this, I had to do the same when my dad died. It sucks, it fucking hurts, and they don't deserve anything from us, but it's still how this goes."

I blow out a heavy breath, my insides feel like they're caving in on me once more. Five minutes ago I was about to tell Vivian I love her. Now this is slamming down on me. "I have a girl. I met a girl."

"I know. Everett told me all about her and I don't know what to say other than the timing of it all sucks."

My eyes close, my voice suffocating in defeat. "When do I fly out?"

"I have you booked on a flight from Hartford tomorrow. You

fly directly to Dublin and then a car and driver will be there to take you wherever you need to go."

"Tomorrow? That's too soon."

"I'm sorry. I can't do anything about that. I'll email you the details."

It's not his fault and I know better than anyone that he's right. That's how this works. The law is the law, even when someone you hate and want no part of dies. I don't care about his money, and I intend to donate every bloody cent to women's charities throughout Ireland and the world. But more than not wanting to deal with this business, I don't want to leave Vivian. It's too soon and I'm far from ready.

A voice in my head asks, *yeah, but will you ever be ready?*

No. And I can't decide if this makes it easier or harder. If dragging out the hours and days with her would have made this worse. I want Vivian's love. I want her heart. But I have no way of keeping them.

Regardless, it doesn't sound like I have a choice now.

"Tomorrow then. Thanks for letting me know. See ye soon, mate." I disconnect the call and let the phone slip through my fingers, falling to the bed beside my head with a gentle thud. I don't have the clearest picture of my father in my head anymore. Mostly because I did what I could to wipe it clean of him.

A man who knocked his wife and occasionally his boy around did not deserve to die in any sort of wealth or comfort. My finger glides along the scar through my eyebrow. He gave me this and that was the final straw for mam. We moved three days later with only the clothes on our backs. I don't even care if it makes me a bad man to hope it hurt and he was scared right before the end took him.

Because of him, I had to leave Ireland. Because of him, I had no one when mam died. Because of him, I had a shitty fucking childhood.

A slight tap at the door, but I don't move.

"Cian?" Vivian's soft voice slips through me like a tonic. "Is everything okay?"

"C'mere to me." I hold my arm out in the air for her. Her sweet body covers mine, her head resting over my ravaged heart. My fingers toy with her hair, twirling the silky strands around and around. She lets me stay like this, silently holding her until I grow a pair and say, "I have to leave tomorrow."

She stiffens. "How come?"

"My da died. Evidently I'm his only living family member and I have to be the one to settle his estate."

"Oh, Cian. I'm so very sorry."

"Don't be sorry. He was a miserable piece of gobshite, and I've hated him since practically the day I was born. I'm upset because I don't want to leave ye. Not yet." Not ever.

She squeezes me. "I don't want you to leave yet either. I want you to stay and never go." A sigh. "I'm sorry. I know that's selfish and wrong to say, but I can't help it."

And there it is. Yet another reason for me to hate my da more. He's taking me from her.

"Vivian, I don't know what to say or do about us. I want ye, darlin'. I want ye like mad. I don't want anyone else. I think yer it for me. I know that might sound crazy, but it's where my heart and mind are. But I don't know how to ask any of that of ye. I'm gone for four months, living in a glorified trailer with three other men. Yer trying to figure your own life out. Yer own path."

"I know. I didn't expect to feel like this for you either. Certainly not so fast."

Her cracked words pierce my heart, splitting it in two.

I can't handle the thought of never seeing her again. Never touching her or smelling her or kissing her or holding her. "Yer my heart." It's all I can say without falling to pieces. I've already damn near cried once today.

"And you're my soul."

"But I can't stay and ye can't go with me."

"No."

My lungs empty on a shuddered exhale. Losing mam was excruciating. This feels worse somehow. This feels like a future of possibility and happiness slipping through my fingers like tiny grains of sand.

"I'm not giving up on us. And my heart will never let ye go."

16

VIVIAN

They say that when life hands you lemons, make lemonade. Only that's bullshit. When life hands you lemons, trade that shit in for some premium vodka, a box of mixed chocolates, and add a nice dollop of fuck you world on top.

Cian left right after lunch today.

He wouldn't let me drive him to the airport. He said if I was there saying goodbye, he'd never be able to get on the plane. I was honestly—okay selfishly—hoping he wouldn't get on the plane but then Peter the booger reminded me that if he wasn't leaving today, he was leaving regardless.

We said we wouldn't say goodbye, thinking it would be better that way. That if we didn't say it then we wouldn't break, and it wouldn't be real. That maybe we'd be able to go back to life as it was before. But what was life before?

I had said I wanted to be a Samantha and not a Charlotte. I had said I wanted adventure and to stop living so rigidly by the rules of others. And for a brief moment, six blissfully short days, I did that. All of it. I laughed and I danced and I fucked and I loved and I let go.

I lived.

And in living, I discovered all I'd been doing before that was existing.

Not even six days of perfection and I'm like Little Orphan Annie. All by myself. Again. No wait, that's not what that song is from nor does that analogy make any sense. "Alexa, play depressing music." It's not even like I can say play depressing breakup music because we didn't break up. You'd have to actually be with someone in order to break up.

And of course, because the universe is out for my blood, Alexa starts playing one of Reckless Motion's flipping ballads with Cian's crooning voice coming through.

"Alexa, you suck at life, and I hope you die a horrible electronic death."

"I'm sorry, I don't know that one," she replies in that obnoxiously polite robotic voice.

"Yeah, I just bet you don't," I grumble, polishing off the last of my martini.

"Is it the rock star or the man?"

I roll my eyes at Hazel. "I didn't even know he was a rock star when I met him. Him being famous and a rock star is actually one of the things I like least about him. Him being a rock star is why he's gone and not here with me now. Women are all over him. If his damn IG page isn't enough of an indication of that, I saw it the night we met in the airport. Our waitress was hoping he'd tell her to drop to her knees and unzip his pants every time she asked him if she could get him anything else."

"Okay. So the rock star part of his life sucks. But he seemed like a genuine, normal guy when he was here."

"That's because I think that's who he is. Music is his passion. The rest of the stuff just comes along with him."

"Right. It's a lot to take on," my mother says. "Certainly not for the faint of heart. Do you love him?"

That's my mom for you. Always bringing it back to basics.

Thankfully in the spirit of true sisterhood, both Hazel and my mother are drinking with me. It's not like it takes much to get them to do that, so it wasn't much of an ask. Never a good idea to drink your misery alone. That's how you end up waking up in a pool of your own vomit on the bathroom floor. I saw that once in a *Lifetime* movie. The girl ended up in the hospital with alcohol poisoning. Not a good look on her and not one I want for myself.

"Love." I blow a raspberry at no one in particular. "Blah. Who would ever be stupid enough to fall in love with a sexy Irishman with sexy dimples?"

"You said sexy twice."

"What are you, my copy editor, Hazel? Back off. He is sexy. Every sexy thing about him is sexy. Even the sexy was sexy."

My mother sighs. "Why aren't you going with him again?" She finishes off her martini and pours us another round that's sitting ready and fired up in the chilled shaker.

"Because he's living on a tour bus with three other dudes for four months. Women aren't invited along. In fact, given who they are and what they're out in the world doing, we're likely discouraged."

"So what's your plan then, Viv?"

I throw my hands up at my mother for asking such a question at such a time. Clearly the answer is right in front of her face. "Drink myself into a stupor, sleep with his pillow so I can smell him one last time, and then tomorrow wake up and figure out a real and sustainable plan for my life."

"Wow, that sounds so boring."

"Thanks, Hazel. I know, but what the hell else am I going to do?" I take a massive gulp of my martini that's tasting more and more like water and less and less like cosmo.

"Does Hunter enter into that at all?"

"No. He does not."

My father smiles with approval and when did he get here or

was he here the whole time? And did he hear every word I said about the sexy being sexy? Things are a bit fuzzy. Like the room that's tipping this way and that.

"I think I should have some real food before I end up barfing up chocolate and then can never eat it again."

Hazel nods solemnly. "That's me with spaghetti." She gags at the thought of it. "Have you ever puked up freaking spaghetti? It's the worst."

"I ordered pizza twenty minutes ago," my mom states and then gestures toward my martini glass. "Finish that up because that's the last one you're getting. And after pizza we're making popcorn and watching *Encanto* with Willow and Penny. This is the official end of your pity party."

"Party pooper," I grumble, but do as I'm told all the same. Because truth, I've never been all that great at feeling sorry for myself. I'm not a huge wallower. So after pizza and popcorn and *Encanto* with my nieces who know every word to every song and sing along at top volume, I trudge up the steps to the room I shared with Cian all week.

It no longer feels like mine.

It feels like ours and the moment I enter and catch the faint trace of his cologne all my bravado crumbles along with my face and I succumb to a pile of tears and heartbreak complete with nose-diving into his pillow. I'm not mad or hurt. I don't blame Cian for needing to go. He was never anything but honest with me and I knew the score from the start.

I'm just sad. So very, very sad.

And that's how I fall asleep. A mess of a woman breathing heavily into her lover's pillow only to wake the next morning to a colossal headache and a noise. A noise that's reverberating like a Ping-Pong machine in my skull. *Ping. Ping. Ping.*

"Ugh."

Rolling over, I flop halfway off the bed and paw for my phone, slapping at the nightstand until I'm able to finger it in my direction. Pinching one eye shut, I squint the other open and blearily take in the screen.

Cian.

Cian is texting me.

And while that should have me screaming for joy and excited beyond belief, it has me wary. I mentally said goodbye to him. And with that goodbye, I had intended to put him out of my mind for at least four months. I didn't want thoughts or hope or expectations and desires or anything to impact me. I need to find a new place to live. I need to gather myself and discover what I want next.

But I can't ignore the text either.

Swiping my finger up the screen, I read his texts.

Cian: I wasn't going to text you. I wasn't going to call you either. But I miss you. I'm in the town where I grew up and it's exactly as it was when I left. So little has changed and it's harder to take in than I thought it would be. I have a meeting in an hour with my father's attorney and then the funeral people and I... I'm sorry. All I can think about is how I wish I was in bed, snuggled up with you instead of here.

Cian: I don't know if this is right or wrong or fair or not, but I feel like I left my heart when I left you and now I'm here, alone and empty and hollow.

Cian: You don't have to reply, and you don't have to feel obligated to do it either, but I emailed you something just in case. There are no strings. Use it for this or don't. It's just there so you know where my head and heart are.

Scooching myself up, I sit, drawing my knees up to my chest and rereading his texts. Poor guy, having to deal with all of that. And doing it alone. My heart breaks for him and I wish I was there. I wish I was with him to help him through this.

Then I open my email app on my phone and find two separate emails. One is from either his manager or assistant because when I open the email, it's all very businesslike.

There's a PDF attachment of the band's touring schedule and the email goes on to explain that if I should travel at any point to see the band, to email a woman named Dorothy and she'll arrange for me to have tickets as well as VIP backstage passes.

Then I open the next email and discover a five-thousand-dollar flight gift card.

That part has my eyes bulging from their sockets and the remains of pizza, popcorn, chocolate, and vodka to slosh terribly around in my belly.

Five thousand dollars?

This is clearly his way of saying he wants me to fly out to see him. At least once because damn, I could buy a few tickets with that kind of scratch. Not first class likely, but who gives a shit?

I could ask so many questions. I could have doubts about all of this. He's a seriously famous rock star. He was a total flirt the night we met. He's used to giving people lines and telling women what they want to hear. Those IG pictures of women being all over him are proof enough. The world wants him.

He's also vulnerable and yes, likely feeling lonely and a bit lost. Between Christmas and now this, I know he's been feeling that.

I could use all of that as an explanation for why he latched so quickly on to me. For what these texts are and for what happened between us.

But I don't think any of those reasons are the reason he's this way with me.

I think Cian loves me. I think he was going to tell me so on the couch before we were interrupted. I glance down at the charm bracelet on my wrist. At the platinum Celtic love knot with the emerald in the center. The color of my eyes, he said.

This present wasn't for show. It was a goodbye gift. A don't-forget-me gift.

But could it simply be the start of our story and not the end?

I asked this once before. What happens when two people who might in fact be meant for each other meet at the wrong time? I had claimed then that they move on and find other people and live other lives. But now I wonder if love is able to persevere and triumph, or if it's truly snuffed out in the wake of life and obligations and expectations?

It's a brave thing to throw everything on the line for another without knowing how it will all turn out. But I've already been feeling it, all this time, just as Oscar Wilde said it. *"To live is the rarest thing in the world. Most people exist, that is all."*

I know that's what I've been doing. Existing.

Taking the cleanest, easiest, safest path.

Dating men who are perfect on paper but not in reality. Writing the same type of books without pushing myself to venture in a little deeper. Relying on my family to get me through whenever I hit a bump in the road.

Being with Cian won't be easy. These four months won't be easy.

There will be jealousy and nerves and doubts.

But if we can do this, if we can make this love work...

And then it's there. To the point where I have to close my eyes so I can picture it. It's not an easy story to tell. I'm a plotter but this is a total pantser situation I'm creating. But I think I want to write the question I posed. What *does* happen when two people who live two totally different lives who might in fact be meant for each other meet at the wrong time?

My heart pounds and my sickly belly gives an excited jolt.

Because not only am I going to find out the answer, I'm also going to write the hell out of it.

17

CIAN

Sweat beads on my forehead, dripping down my temples. The heat of the stage lights on me feels especially oppressive tonight. I use my forearm to wipe it away and then the hem of my shirt, drawing a round of whistles and catcalls from the audience. This is our second and last show in Paris. Tomorrow we finally have a blessed day off before we're set to travel to Belgium and then Germany.

It's already been two weeks on the road.

That makes it nearly three weeks since I left Connecticut and not one peep from Vivian.

I know she got my texts. I know she got the emails I had sent to her.

Everett tells me I need to cut my losses, but that feels like giving up and giving up on Vivian isn't something I think I can do. Pathetically, the more days that go by, the more I'm starting to understand and sympathize with Hunter. Which brings up a fresh round of bitterness and brutal jealousy because... Is she in New York? Is she with him?

Part of me wishes I had told her I love her. The other part is relieved I didn't because nothing sucks worse than feeling like a twat for telling a girl you love her when she doesn't reciprocate.

Shifting my acoustic back into place, I strum a few chords. We have a regular set list, but upon reaching the end of the night, I like to mix things up a bit. Keeps the nights from bleeding into the next.

"Play the song," a woman with a thick French accent calls out from somewhere close to the stage. At that, the entire place goes nuts, clapping and cheering.

The song she's talking about is the song I wrote for Vivian and since we started the tour, it's gotten more requests than anything else. It's been laughingly referred to on social media as "the song" since I have yet to title it or even speak about it though it's been asked about loads during interviews we've done.

I've been good about playing it since it made me feel closer to Vivie, but tonight, my heart just isn't in it. Mulling this over, I continue to strum something noncommittal when the same French woman yells, "Tell us about the song. About the girl."

The girl.

I can't tell them about the girl.

I've been apart from her longer than I've known her but instead of the absence growing easier, it's growing harder. My dreams are filled with her. Red hair and sparkling green eyes and idiosyncrasies and beautiful, sweet soul. I keep the picture she made for me in my bunk, and even though I love having that image of me with mam right there, I can't help but wish it was one of me with Vivie. A permanent reminder that even in its brevity, it was real.

The crowd begins to grow impatient, and my drummer hisses out, "Just play it, man."

So I do.

I play the song I wrote for her, starting to hate the lyrics more and more for their mocking my pain and reminder of time running out. The fans go wild for it, and that's how we close out the night. But the high isn't there. The joy and thrill in my life are now flat and textureless. The prism of color and shape I had before is gone and in its place is a vacuous chasm.

It's bloody awful and nothing short of torture.

Tied up in knots over a woman I hardly knew feels ridiculous, but I can't shake it all the same.

I fly off the stage, anxious to clean up and sleep most of tomorrow away. But the second I round the corner, finding my way through the dark with the deafening rumble of clapping as my backdrop, I hear my security detail arguing with someone.

"It's fake, ma'am. I'm not sure what else to say. You're not going back there."

"It's not fake," the woman insists. "I got this from their assistant, Dorothy."

"No VIP backstage passes were handed out as the band gave strict instructions. No groupies."

"I'm not a groupie, you booger. That song Cian just played was about me."

"Uh-huh. Sure it was. You and every other woman on the planet."

"Can you please just listen to me? I flew in to surprise—"

"Vivie?" I'm hopping over the first security checkpoint and bounding for the second before I even know how I got here.

"Cian?"

Jesus. It really is her. I slam into Lawrence, who is probably twice my weight and size, shoving him half out of the way to get to her. "Yer here?"

"I'm here." She gives me a smile that lights up my soul and charges my blood, making me feel edgy. Wired. Alive.

Her red hair is down in thick, glossy waves. Her green eyes lined in dark makeup with something shimmery on the lids. Her lips match her hair, and never has a woman looked more stunning than mine.

I reach for her, my fingers itching for contact, only for her to get tossed aside, stumbling and falling to the ground as another woman comes at me. "He's mine," she screams, and then she's yelling things in French I can't quite make out since my French is about as limited as my ability to speak any other language fluently. Not to mention my accent doesn't do the French language any justice.

"Vivian," I yell, going for the metal barrier to try and get to her, only now Lawrence isn't fucking around. He's moving me back step by step and telling another security guy to clear the scene. "No. That's her. That's my girlfriend. You have to let me get her."

"I'm sorry, sir. I can't let you—"

Fuck this. I duck under his elbow and sprint to the metal barrier, jumping over it and finding Vivian just as she gets herself back up to her feet. The other woman as well as several other fans swarm us, snapping pictures and taking videos and asking for autographs and yelling questions.

My arms wrap around Vivian, and I tuck her into my chest, shielding her as best I can while I trudge through the clamoring horde. Thankfully my security surrounds us, blocking access to us as we reach the other side of the barrier, and then I'm gripping her hand and running up the stairs and through the back area to the greenroom at the far end of the building.

I spin her through the door and slam it shut behind us, taking her into the bright and slightly blinding light, only to realize we're not alone. My bandmates are sipping on drinks and munching on the food left in here.

"Vivian, these are my bandmates and friends. Guys, this is Vivian, the one I've been a miserable sack of moaning shite over. Now that you've all been introduced, get the fuck out of here so I can be alone with my woman."

Each one gives her a hug, telling her how happy they are to finally meet her and how glad they are that she showed up.

Who cares? Out. That's all I can think. I need them gone. And the second they are, my hands are up in Vivian's hair, as I wanted them to be before, and my mouth is covering hers.

I spin us around and walk her into the door, locking it soundly and pressing her into the wood. "Yer here?"

She laughs into me. "I am."

"I hadn't heard from ye. I thought that meant—"

Her fingers rake through my hair. "I'm sorry. I wanted to get in touch. I wanted to call or text. I missed you so much. But I didn't know what to say and I had a lot of soul searching to do. I needed to figure out the things I wanted and didn't want. The things I could tolerate and the things I couldn't. I flew out to LA and spent a few days out there, seeing if it would ever be a fit for me."

"Ye did?" My eyes are wide and wild on hers.

She nods, gnawing on her lip, suddenly nervous. "I'm not insinuating or even expecting you to want to move in with me or even that you want me to move out there, but—"

I stifle her words with another searing kiss. "Vivian, I want ye. I want ye to find a place with me and have it be our place. I want ye to move out to LA, and I want ye to be my fucking girl." My forehead drops to hers, my hands now on her face, holding her. "I love you. I fell in love with you before yer pretty eyes even met mine. It was first bloody sight, and I don't even care if people say that's impossible because it's not. They're not feeling this. There is no other word in the human language to describe how I feel about ye other than to call it love. Which, if ye think about it, is immensely limiting. I think as an author ye should come up with something grander."

"I'm working on it," she says with a small giggle at my exuberance. "I'm writing our story, Cian. That's also what I've been doing these weeks. I'm writing our love story. I just don't know how it's going to end yet."

I smile into her eyes, rubbing my nose along hers. "Ah,

darlin', that's easy. It doesn't. True love stories never end, especially ones like ours."

My mouth attacks hers in an urgent frenzy, my hands tearing at her dress, pulling it up and over her head. She makes quick work of my clothes too and within seconds I have her lifted in my arms and pinned against the door and then I'm inside of her. Pounding her into the door like a madman, but this is a rock concert and I'm fairly certain I'm not the first rock star to fuck a woman backstage.

Only she's not just some woman. She's my woman and I tell her that, over and over again. I tell her how I love her. How miserable and heartbroken I've been since the moment I left her. I tell her how these four months won't be easy, but that we'll make it work however we can and that she has me. That I will never be anyone else's because I will only, ever want her.

"I love you too," she pants into my mouth, her body wrapped around me like a vine. "So much. I've never felt this for anyone else. It's you, Cian. It'll always be you. Forever. My heart will only ever be yours."

"Yes," I hiss as her words shoot me higher, closer. I need to be deeper inside her. I need to feel and touch and love every inch of this woman from the inside out. I want to mark her with my cum and one day feel my child grow inside of her.

All that emptiness that sat on my chest and in my heart is filled up with her. A woman I never saw coming but now couldn't imagine my life without.

She comes with a muffled cry, a shudder overtaking her, and I hate that we're still trying to keep it quiet. "Tonight, I'm taking you to a hotel, renting the fucking penthouse, and ye can scream yer bloody lungs out all ye want. No more hiding, darlin'. Never again."

My orgasm slams through me as her pussy continues to spasm around me, milking everything from me. I collapse against her, pressing her deeper into the door and then I release her, sliding out and cleaning her up with a clean towel they have for us in here. We get dressed and then I'm taking her hand, leading her out the door, and away from the stadium. My security is all around us, leading us through a private entrance at the back.

"Where to, sir?" Lawrence asks once we're in the back of a car.

"To a hotel that has a soundproof penthouse," I tell him, smiling at Vivian's laugh. "How long are ye staying?" I ask her.

She shrugs at me. "To be determined, but probably not that long. But don't worry, I'll be back. I already booked tickets to four other places along your tour."

I drag her head to my shoulder, my lips pressing into her hair while I breathe in her scent. "We're really doing this."

"We're really doing this," she agrees.

"And LA?"

"That too."

"Ye won't regret it. I'll spend my life making sure of it."

"The only thing I would have regretted was not taking the chance." Her eyes meet mine. "But I think we're worth all the risk life has to throw at us."

"We're worth everything and as long as we have each other, we have everything. Forever and always. That's gonna be us."

EPILOGUE

VIVIAN

The following December 20th

"Are you ready for this?" I ask Cian as he pulls the rental car into my parents' driveway and puts it in park.

He turns to me, his brows creased in confusion and concern. "What are ye so nervous about? You've been on edge ever since we left LA."

I glance toward my parents' house, decorated in gold lights, and then back to him. "It's like déjà vu. I don't know. All of this makes me edgy."

He grins, leaning in and gliding his nose along mine. "Ye think Hunter is going to be here vying fer yer love and affection and I'm going to have to pretend I'm yer man to fend him off?"

"Pretend?" I challenge.

"See what I'm saying then? Ye have nothing to be nervous about and this is so much better than déjà vu because anywhere I go, ye come too. And vice versa."

"I know. I'm fine." I sag and sigh. "I'm being crazy."

"Yer not crazy. Yer beautiful." He kisses me, hands in my hair holding me close and erasing the nerves I can't seem to shake. "Ye think yer da will let us share a bed this time?"

I smile against his lips. "Now that we're actually together? No way."

"He managed well enough when they came out to LA and stayed with us. If it helps, I can tell him you still like being on top."

I smack his shoulder, making him laugh.

"Come on, darlin'. Let's get our bags and get inside where it's warm. One thing I don't miss about the East Coast is the weather." He gives an exaggerated shudder and then he turns off the car and gets out, popping the trunk to retrieve our bags.

I get out too, my heart thundering as I climb up the front steps to the house. So much has happened in the last year. I ended up traveling to Europe and Asia to see Cian and his band play six times instead of only four. Their third album was a huge success, plus the EP of the song he wrote for me skyrocketed them into the music stratosphere. They're going to add it to their fourth album which releases in a couple of months.

We made it through the tour together.

Stronger than ever and then we found a place in LA.

Once word got out about my and Cian's relationship, my book sales jumped to a new level. Especially when I released the story I wrote about us. It hit the *New York Times* bestseller list and has been sitting in the top one hundred on every channel for over a month now.

It's been incredible.

A whirlwind of award shows and paparazzi and security. And love. So much love. I can't get enough of Cian. I'm just hoping this trip home proves to be relaxing for both of us. Frankly, we need the break and downtime.

Cian takes my hand, our suitcase in his other, and his guitar on his back. He gives me that smile. The one with dimples and white teeth that never fails to make my heart sprint and my belly swoop.

"Happy birthday, Vivie Girl." He leans in and kisses me just as the door swings open.

"Tongue out of my daughter's mouth, Cian," my father says, his tone stern though his hint of a smile gives him away.

"Yes, sir." Cian pulls away, releasing my hand so he can shake my father's. "Good to see ye, Theo."

My dad hauls Cian in for a hug and every time that happens, I fight the urge to break into tears. Cian has no family but mine and the way they have embraced him as theirs means everything. Both to me and to Cian.

"Welcome home, son. We're glad you're both finally here."

And yup, there is no stopping the tears now. I sniffle, attempting to hide them, but Cian hears, and I'm busted.

"Aw, darlin'. No tears." Cian grabs me, pulling me into his side and kissing the top of my head.

"They're happy tears," I promise, sniffling some more into his shirt as I get myself under control.

"Since when are you this emotional?" my father asks, dragging me out of Cian's arms and into his.

"We'll blame Christmas. And you called him son."

My father chuckles softly. "I've always called him son."

"I know!" Another flood of tears comes, and I can practically feel my father rolling his eyes at Cian. "Don't mock me, Daddy. I'm a romance author. We're emotional people."

"So it seems. Happy birthday, baby girl. Your mother and Hazel are in the kitchen making birthday dinner and cake and Peter and the girls are in the dining room playing poker."

I pull away, tilting my head. "Did you say poker?"

My father nods and this time he does in fact roll his eyes. "Yes. Peter thought it would be a good idea to teach them poker. And blackjack because there's math involved. Only the little demons are card sharks. Good thing we were playing for change and not bills, or I'd have to sell the house to cover my losses."

"Yeesh."

Cian sets everything down and follows me into the kitchen, giving my mother and Hazel a hug. They pepper us with a million and six questions and upon hearing us, Peter and the girls come into the kitchen. Both Penny and Willow attack Cian, jumping on him and naturally, kicking him in the junk again.

Cian falls to the floor in a pained groan, huffing and puffing.

"You might want to start wearing a cup. I have."

"Cheers, mate," Cian groans. "I'll consider that for next time."

"Why is Cian's face red?" Willow asks.

"Because he's holding his breath, so he doesn't throw up all over Grandma's floor," Hazel tells her.

"Oh no." Willow jumps on him, rubbing his face and pulling his hair. "Whenever I throw up, mommy has to hold my hair over the potty. Do you want me to do that for you?"

"He's fine." I pick her up off him, spinning my little redheaded niece around. "He just needs a couple more minutes and he'll be up and off the floor."

"Can we come back to your house in Caluferna again?" Penny begs, jumping up and down. "I want to swim in your pool. Cian can play shark again."

"This spring, honey, we'll go back out to California for a visit," Peter tells Penny.

"Yay!" Both girls scream and run out of the room.

"I swear, they're getting harder and harder to corral." Hazel gives an exhausted sigh, picking at the cheese platter on the kitchen counter. "I thought having babies and toddlers was tough, but the older they get, the harder it's been."

"You alright, baby?" I ask, rubbing Cian's back.

"Grand. Just bloody grand. Hope ye didn't want babies anytime soon, darlin' because my bollocks might be out of commission for the rest of my life." He slowly peels himself up and off the floor with Peter's help. They've become friends somewhat in the last year.

I snort out a laugh that sounds like more of a deranged hiccup. "I think we'll be set on that for a while."

Cian drops a kiss on my cheek.

"You want a drink, Cian? I'm guessing you could use a whiskey after that." My mom starts pouring Cian about five fingers of whiskey into a crystal tumbler before handing it to him.

"Ah, thank you, Darla. That's perfect." He holds it up to her in salute and then takes a sip. "Merry Christmas."

"Merry Christmas yourself," my mother replies. "When are you going to make an honest woman out of my daughter?"

"Mom!" I screech while Cian chokes on his whiskey. "You can't ask questions like that. It's... intrusive and frankly awkward."

My mother waves me away. "I'm a grandmother, Vivian, I can do whatever the fuck I want to at this stage of the game."

"Ugh."

I throw Cian an apologetic look that makes him smile and wink at me.

"Well, the cake has another fifteen minutes or so to bake and I'm parched. Cheese and cocktails, anyone?" my mother asks, already taking it upon herself to start filling the large martini shaker with ice and flavored vodkas.

"Oh, me! Yes!" Hazel grabs the cheese platter and walks it into the dining room and the rest of us follow her. "Try this cheese, Viv. It's to die for. We brought it with us from Brooklyn. There is the best cheese shop that opened around the corner from our apartment. It's a raw goat cheese with hints of truffle in it."

I stare at the cheese. "Um. Maybe later."

I get a bunch of eyes for that, and a cold sweat breaks out on the back of my neck. "Maybe later? You love goat cheese. It's your favorite," Peter challenges.

"I know."

"Here. I'll make you a cracker. Just try it. I promise, you'll go crazy for it." Haze slices into it and lathers it on a piece of lavash before shoving it at me. I take it from her hand and smile. Thankfully my mother comes in, only this isn't going to get any better for me. It's only going to get worse, and I shouldn't have waited.

It was stupid of me to think I could.

"Here darlings. Take." My mother hands me a martini glass filled with pink liquid. "It's that berry cosmo thing we made last year. I've perfected it. It's delish."

"You've perfected it because you drink it nearly three times a week," my father teases.

"How are you supposed to perfect something if you don't practice, Theo? If I never made it or drank it, this one wouldn't be very good and then what kind of mother and hostess would I be?"

"Straight facts," Hazel agrees, taking a huge sip of hers only to chase it down with cheese. "Besides, I'm a much better mother after I've had one of these."

We all laugh, and my mother holds up her drink. "To Christmas and my family being home for it."

"To Christmas," we repeat, holding up our glasses and clinking them.

"What the hell is going on here?" my mother snaps, her eyes on me. "Vivian, you didn't take a sip."

"And she hasn't tried my cheese either. Something isn't right. You're not drinking or eating... oh shit. You're pregnant."

Fuck.

My mother gasps and pounds down the rest of her martini.

"What?" That's my dad, Peter, and Cian together.

"Yer pregnant?" Cian is now standing beside me, his drink on the table forgotten as he stares incredulously at me. "Is that true?"

"He didn't know?" It's Hazel's turn to gasp now. "Oh, double shit."

"Um. Well." I glance around at my family who are all staring at me and then back to Cian. "Yes. I was going to tell you on Christmas morning. I had this whole thing planned out, but that was stupid, right? I should have known I wouldn't make it through the alcohol gauntlet that is Christmas with my family without everyone finding out."

"Yer pregnant." He says it again, only this time it's not a question.

I start to gnaw on my lip, shifting my weight from one foot to the other. This isn't exactly the reaction I was expecting from him, and I can't read his face. It's like a mask of stone. What do I say? I've already told him yes. He's mad though. And I get it. I mean, this isn't how I wanted him to find out. Not in front of my family like this.

"I should have told you sooner. I should have told you when it was just us. I wanted it to be a surprise and then—" My hands cover my face and I start to shake, my chin quivering and damn these stupid pregnancy emotions. I'm only like six weeks along, but hell if they're not already getting the best of me. "I found out two days ago, and I thought it would make a perfect Christmas present. I'm sorry. I'm so sorry."

"Maybe we should give them some privacy," my father suggests as the room grows eerily quiet.

"That won't be necessary, Theo," Cian says. "What I have to say to Vivian, I'd like to say in front of all of you."

I'm being pushed down into a chair, Cian's hands now on my shoulders and I can't look at him. Even as he pries my hands from my face. I stare down at my lap. He kneels before me, his hands cupping my face and dragging my gaze up to his just as the first of my tears slips. His thumb is there, brushing it away, but more start to fall and the attempt is futile.

He gives me a soft smile, his ice-blue eyes all over me. "Why are ye cryin', darlin'? I'm not mad or upset."

"You're not?" I croak.

He shakes his head. "Nah. Shocked, yeah. I certainly didn't expect that."

"You looked upset."

His smile grows as he rubs his nose against mine. It's his thing. His love pet and it never fails to calm everything inside me while anchoring me firmly to him. "No. I'm not upset. It just sped this all up. Ye see, I wasn't going to give ye this until Christmas morning, but now that I know yev got my baby in yer belly, I can't wait."

Another round of gasps as Cian places a small wooden box on my lap. Then he leans in and kisses my still flat belly and I think I die. I know I cry a hell of a lot more.

"What is this?" I ask when he makes no move to do anything else.

He nudges it higher up my thigh. "Open it."

I take off the square top and push around the white tissue paper that's inside. Nestled at the bottom on a small velvet pillow is a huge diamond, the platinum band on either side of the stone twisted like the Celtic love knot he gave me on my charm bracelet last year.

"Oh, Cian."

Reaching in, he pulls out the ring and slides it on my finger. "Vivie Girl, yev had my heart wrapped around yours since the first second I saw ye just one year ago. One year, Vivie, and it's been the best of my life. I've traveled the world and I've seen so many things. But of all the places I've been and the things I've done, I'm nowhere without you. Marry me, darlin'. Spend yer life with me. Give us babies and smiles and joy. And I swear to ye, I'll give ye everything. Every piece of me is yours. Forever and always."

My face falls forward, my forehead pressing against his. "Yes. I'll marry you. Forever and always," I repeat to him. It's been our promise to each other. One I know we'll keep for the rest of our lives.

"Yer giving me a family." His voice cracks and I feel him tremble against me.

"We're giving us a family."

His lips slam into mine, his hands tangled up in my hair as we consume each other. More tears fall. Mine and his. But it's mixed with smiles and laughter and a lot of "I can't believe we're having a baby." Mostly, I can't believe this is us. That one crazy night in an airport bar got us here.

I guess it's true what they say. That love comes from the most unexpected places at the most unexpected times. But there is nothing about our story I'd change. And it's only getting started.

The End.

Thank you for reading my fun and steamy Christmas story. Vivian and Cian were so much fun to write. If you want to see more of Vivian and Cian, they pop up in Irresistibly Perfect. Keep reading for the first two chapters of it!

Thanks again!!! XO

Want another free Christmas book? Scan the code!

IRRESISTIBLY PERFECT

CHAPTER 1

A noise stirs me awake and I groan, rolling over on the bed, and stuffing my head back under the pillow. It's too early to wake up. I don't even know what time it is, I just know it's too damn early. Fallon flew into Chicago for my concert and then we spent all last night talking, not going to bed until about four in the morning.

Even then I didn't want to go to bed.

Sleep feels like such a waste of precious minutes when I get so few with her.

That thought has me groaning again, flopping over onto my back, and reluctantly blinking my eyes open. My hotel suite is painfully bright, and I immediately snap my eyes shut against the blinding morning rays of sunshine flowing through the open curtains.

"Fall Girl?" I call out because that noise had to be her. She refused to sleep in the bed with me, even when I told her I'd be good and not touch her. It's not the first time we've seen each other and not fucked, and despite what she thinks, I am capable of controlling myself.

Barely.

Wanting Fallon Lark and not being able to have her has been the story of my life since I was fourteen. She was the girl next door. Her family moving in without having any clue about the fucked-up nightmare that lived beside them in the pretty old mansion. One night, I was sitting on my rooftop, staring across the Charles River at the twinkling lights of Boston while strumming on my guitar when she climbed up and joined me, introducing herself to me as a girl I can never be friends with, but that she'll always regret not getting to know me.

That's what she said, and I was instantly intrigued.

Plus, she was fucking beautiful.

There was no denying that part of it. I looked at her and my heart spun wildly in my chest. She sat there with me for hours that summer night, listening to me play and sing, talking to me about the books she loved to read and how one day she wanted to see the world country by country by getting lost in each one. She wanted to be a doctor, she wanted to save lives and make a difference—the one thing she did manage to do for herself since she's now officially a doctor, starting her residency in Miami as a pediatrician.

It wasn't until the next day that I realized the reality of our situation.

I met her twin brother Dillon and instantly became best friends with him—well, at least until a life-changing accident made us enemies. He, I could talk to. He, I could be friends with because every guy has that one friend that your parents hate but overlook because they know you will outgrow him soon enough.

Her, not so much.

The daughter of an extremely wealthy and influential senator and an old money heiress, her life had already been mapped out for her. A good girl who was not allowed to spend time with let alone get wrapped up in the bad boy filled with rock star dreams.

That hasn't stopped us from being friends all these years and it hasn't stopped us from meeting up, usually with her coming to watch my shows like she did last night.

As long as it's all in secret, of course.

Her family can still never know about our friendship. Certainly not how our friendship occasionally blurs lines and becomes more.

"Fall?" I try again when I don't get a response and I don't hear her moving about. Maybe she left to go get coffee or breakfast? I hate that she forced me into the bed when she took the couch. She probably slept like crap on that thing. Dragging myself up and out of bed, I go into the bathroom to wash my face and brush my teeth. My next show is in Indiana tomorrow night and I'm grateful for the night off tonight. I've been touring for six straight months, and it's been night after night after night.

Maybe I can convince Fall to stay with me tonight.

This might be my last chance to spend time with her for a while. I have to imagine being a resident will eat up all of her time. Still, I couldn't be prouder of her.

Heading back into the bedroom, I pull on a pair of joggers and then go in search of Fallon. The living room is empty, the couch where she slept all made up, blankets folded with pillows placed neatly on top.

But that's not what's stopping my breath.

Her stuff is gone. The small suitcase she had with her is nowhere to be found. Neither is her purse. Did she leave without saying goodbye?

No. It can't be. Fall wouldn't do that. She'd never do that.

I stare at the pillow she used, running my hands through my hair only to grip it at the roots. Is this why she was adamant about sleeping on the couch and having me sleep in the bed? So she could run out on me?

I spin, ready to grab my phone from my nightstand and call

her when something catches my eye. My name. Scrawled at the top of a piece of hotel stationary sitting in the center of the desk. No, not just one piece of paper. There are several. My heart starts pounding, a merciless, vicious storm banging painfully against my ribs. I lick my lips, my hands shaking as I snatch the note off the desk.

For a moment, I can't make myself read it.

She's gone without even having said goodbye. This note is her fucking goodbye, and I can't... shit. I just...

Blowing out an uneven breath, I sink down onto the couch she slept on last night, my elbows digging into my parted thighs. It's wet. The pages are wet, stained in her teardrops. Jesus, Fall Girl. What are you doing?

Wiping at my mouth, I pull the note up and begin reading.

Grey,

I stood in the doorway of the bedroom and watched you sleep for entirely too long this morning. I haven't slept. Not a wink. I listened as you fell asleep and that's when my tears started. We've been dancing around this thing between us for years. Years of a friendship no one in my life could know about. Years of coming together the way lovers do when that was never a possibility for us.

Even before Dillon's accident, my parents made it clear they thought you were trouble and that I needed to stay away from you. I tried. Sort of. I wasn't very good at it. I'd go all day long ignoring you in the halls at school and then I'd get home and stare out my window at yours and wonder what you were doing. If you were playing music or doing your homework or messing around with a girl. I'd miss you. I'd miss you like crazy.

I'd sneak into your room at night, and we'd talk for hours, and then sometimes, I'd fall asleep beside you. I'd climb up onto your roof when it was warm out and you'd play for me. We'd call or text whenever we could, using secret aliases in our phones so my parents wouldn't know. I never laughed with anyone the way I laughed with you. I never talked to or shared my secrets with anyone other than you. You were my person.

The only one in my life who ever listened to me. No one cared about the thoughts in my head. No one, except for you.

We were two lost and lonely souls who found each other. Who saw each other. Who understood each other. Your friendship was everything to me. Sometimes it felt like the only real thing in my life. The only thing that was true and just for me.

Then Dillon's accident happened, and everything got worse. My parents blamed you. You blamed yourself. It went from us not being able to be friends to me not being able to even know you or speak to you. Your friendship became even more forbidden to me than it already was.

That didn't stop me from holding on to you when you left to become a huge rock star with Central Square and it didn't stop me when you became a solo artist after. Until now. Until I stand here like a coward writing you a letter because I don't have the guts to say any of this to your face. I knew I'd never be able to do it and I have to do it. I have to.

Even though it breaks my heart, I have to say goodbye. To you. To our friendship. To all of it. Last night was the last time you'll see me. I won't randomly show up at any more of your concerts. I won't call or text. I won't seek you out. It has to be like this. A clean break. A severing of my heart.

Always know your worth. Always know how incredible you are, not just as an artist but as you. The best person I've ever known. I'm so, so proud of you and all you've accomplished. You're forever in my heart and eternally my best friend. Even if our time together ends like this. In another life, you're everything I'd ever want.

Take care of yourself.

All my love,
Your Fall Girl

With my heart in my throat, I ball up the pages in my fist. I'm sick. Furious. Suffocating under the crushing weight of this blow.

Why? Why now? Why after all these years?

Yes, we were impossible. As friends. As lovers. As anything. A perfect Lark princess, she'd never go against her family for me.

I knew that. I always knew that.

She's right. We were secret friends. Friends who had fake names on each other's phones but would still call and text each other constantly. Friends who would only hang out at night after she'd sneak out of her house and into mine. But that friendship was constant and everywhere. A vital source that got me through the hardest moments of my life.

It's why I never told her how much I love her. How in love with her I've always been. There was no shot at us, and I protected my heart from that level of rejection. But that didn't exactly keep me away.

Her either.

For her it was friendship. For me, it was always something else. Especially as we've gotten older and had our stolen moments.

What the fuck, Fallon? She didn't have to do this. She didn't have to fucking do this.

"What the fuck, Fallon?!" I repeat aloud, my voice shredded. *In another life, you're everything I'd ever want.* "Dammit! No!"

Why can't it be this life? Why can't we have each other? Why can't it be us?

I can't lose her. I love her, and I've already lost so much. No. Not gonna happen.

Shooting off the couch, I fly into the bedroom, tearing through my clothes and throwing on a shirt and sneakers. I find my wallet and phone and stuff both into the pockets of my joggers and then I sprint out the door, down the elevator, onto the street, and into the hotel car.

The drive to the airport through Chicago traffic takes forever and I can't handle it. I'm restless. Edgy. Needing to move instead of sitting still and being patient, I call her phone, but it instantly goes to voice mail, and I hang up. I can't leave a message. I can't do this over the phone. I have to find her, and I have to tell her.

Years and years of loving and pining for her.

After an eternity, we reach the airport and then I'm waiting in line and dodging curious glances from people wondering what I'm doing waiting in line at the airport or questioning if it is in fact me. One of the eternal downfalls of being a celebrity is being recognized, and right now I'm in no mood for any of it.

I just want to catch her plane. I just want to get my girl back.

Finally, I reach the counter only to learn I've missed her flight. "The next flight to Miami leaves in three hours," the woman behind the podium says to me.

"I can't wait three hours. Is there another airline?"

"Let me check."

Click, click, click, her nails on the keyboard drive my already frazzled nerves straight to the edge. "Yes, there's a flight that leaves in thirty minutes."

"Put me on it."

"You won't have enough time—"

"Put. Me. On. It. Please," I tack on at the end.

She scowls at my shitty tone and attitude but does as I ask. More clicking and then I hand her my black Amex and license and then a minute later, she's handing me a first-class ticket. I didn't even ask her for that. I would have sat in the fucking bathroom to get on that flight.

"Thank you."

"You'll have to run."

"I plan on it."

And I do. I race through security, apologizing to everyone in the PreCheck line I blow past. With nothing on me, I get through quickly and then I'm going as fast as my legs will carry me through the airport until I reach the gate, sweating and panting for my life, my lungs burning.

I make the flight, just barely, but I'm here and I sag into the leather seat, my eyes closing. My mind drifts, replaying everything from last night. Everything we talked about. I can't pinpoint it. Other than her refusing to get physical, I can't pinpoint a moment where I felt like something was off or that this was a goodbye visit.

She laughed with me. She smiled. We touched and flirted and talked. Hell, we talked about everything and anything. The way we always have.

Not having sex was disappointing, but not out of the ordinary.

In all the years and times we've met up, sometimes we didn't have sex. Sometimes she was just there, holding me and keeping me together when my life was falling apart. Sex was always a byproduct of our friendship. Of our bond and connection.

Her note crinkles in my hand, the sharp edges digging into my fist. I sigh, dragging a restless hand through my hair as I stare out the window at nothing. I'm offered food and drinks from interested flight attendants and I decline everything.

I'm too wound up. Too close to losing my absolute fucking mind.

Why? That's the one thing I don't understand. The one thing that was not explained in the note.

Unfurling it, I read through it again and again, analyzing it. Memorizing it. Every word and swirl of ink I imprint into my brain.

What will I do when she tells me no?

When she looks at me with pity and remorse in her eyes and tells me there is no way we could ever be together?

The plane tracks southeast through the air and by the time we start our descent over Miami, I feel like I'm going down along with us. I created a hundred speeches in my head. Hell, I'd move to Miami if I had to. But as I step off the plane and exit the airport into the blinding hot and humid sun, in my gut I know that won't make a difference.

I power on my phone and stare at it, debating.

It wouldn't be difficult to find her here. A few phone calls at most.

My gut twists painfully, my chest locked in a vise. I slide into the back of a cab, telling the driver to take me to the beach. He recognizes me, instantly chatting me up about my music and a hundred other things I half listen to.

My heart is too exposed, and I duck my head to catch my breath. I left everything behind and impulsively jumped on an airplane and for what? So I can get my heart broken in live action instead of in privacy? So I can demand answers that won't change the outcome of our story and watch as she falls apart?

I know she's hurting. I saw her tears.

This wasn't easy for her, which makes it all the more permanent.

He drops me in front of some posh hotel I never enter. Instead, I head out to the beach, gaze locked on the turbulent water and waves that match my insides. I sink down into the scalding-hot sand, already sweating, and just stare out at the endless ocean.

Her residency, her life, her future, it's all planned out for her. Everything with her family is a strategy. An equation I never fit into. They hate me. They hate my family.

She won't pick me, and I can't ask her to choose me over them. I already know she won't.

That's our reality.

If I love her, I have to let her go. I'm not who she needs. I'm not who anyone needs. A fucked-up bad boy rock star to her perfect princess. I don't deserve her, and I'd only ruin her. Isn't that what Dillon said to me that night so long ago when I confessed everything to him?

In another life, you're everything I'd ever want.

In another life. Just not in this one.

So instead of tracking her down, I sit here. I mourn. I break. And by the time I drag my miserable, sorry ass up and out of the sand and head back to the airport, I vow to let her have the life she's supposed to have. Even if that life isn't with me.

IRRESISTIBLY PERFECT

CHAPTER 2

Three years later

"Can I have your autograph?" the waitress who unsnapped the top two buttons of her uniform after recognizing both me and my older brother asks with a smile that tells me she'd give me anything she could, including her body, if we wanted.

"Sure," I say with a tight grin, mournfully setting down my coffee mug and casting a longing glance at my breakfast. I'm starving, having woken up at 5:00 a.m. with the hope of writing a song this morning. As with every other morning this week I tried to do that, but I came up with nothing. First time in my life this has happened and it's weighing on me.

"Great!" She jumps up and down, practically screaming. "You're my absolute favorite artist. I have all your albums including the Central Square ones." She laughs, batting her eyelashes. "Which I guess means I have your albums too." She points to my brother, Zax with her pen.

"Thank you for that," I tell her genuinely. Hungry or not, a fan is a fan and I fucking love my fans. "That's very sweet of you." I take the pen from her outstretched hand. "What would you like me to sign?"

"My cleavage for sure so I can show my boyfriend later and well…" She searches around as if something is going to materialize before her eyes. "I guess my guest check pad?"

"Um." I have no judgment that she wants me to sign her tits for her boyfriend—that's between them—but we're in a public restaurant, not an after-party or a club. "You're sure about this?"

"Absolutely," she exclaims with a fierce head bob. I shrug and do as the lady asks before handing her pen back. She eyes my handiwork. "Thank you so much. This is amazing. It reminds me of this one time when I came to—"

"We'd like to enjoy our breakfast now," Zax asserts with a gruff yet somehow slightly polite tone.

"Oh." She blushes like a virgin on her wedding night. "Of course. Sure. Enjoy." She shakes her head in a self-deprecating way and then skulks off.

"Thank you," I say to him, finally slicing into my omelet and shoveling a piece into my mouth, stifling my satisfied moan. My stomach was about to start a revolution if I didn't eat in the next ten seconds.

"You have to be harder on them, or they'll think you're easy pickings and drape themselves all over you."

I nod as I chew. "I know," I garble around a mouthful of eggs, spinach, and bacon, washing it down with a sip of my coffee. "But I'm not good at it. Suzie used to tell me that fans are fans and without them, you're nothing—which is true—and that if you start blowing them off or making them feel unimportant, word spreads faster than chlamydia at a frat party that you're a dick."

Zax chokes on his benedict. "Did you have to use the word *chlamydia* while I'm eating?"

I give him an amused look and then continue to devour my eggs.

"You know, if you had a steady girlfriend, women would back off you."

I laugh because truly, that's funny. "You know that's not true. You were a rock star once and had women all over you even though you were with Suzie at the time. It was even worse after she died, and you were mourning. The women who want to fuck a rock star for the sake of fucking a rock star don't care if you or even they are coupled up already. That waitress just had me sign her tits and she has a boyfriend. Besides, there is no one out there I'd want to date."

"You sure about that?"

"Which part?" I retort cheekily and he rolls his eyes at me. "Yes, matchmaker Jane, I'm sure. What is this? Because you've found someone again you must make sure the rest of us do too? Monogamy doesn't fit with my lifestyle right now," I tell my brother, chowing down on toast this time. "I'm coming off my most successful album yet. Eden Dawson, my producer, and Lyric Rose, my record company exec told me it's also my *best* yet. I have to follow that up, make the next album even better." I subdue the rising panic with that thought. "I have to tour to promote my music, which means I'm traveling for weeks or months all the time. Dating doesn't jive well with that. As it is, I spend too much time getting hit on for simply being Greyson Monroe. That's not what I want in a woman and until I meet the perfect one, it's a big fat hard pass on dating."

Zax laughs. A real laugh, which for Zax is saying a lot. He lost Suzie who was his girlfriend, the woman he was going to propose to when she had a stroke in the shower. A stroke at the age of twenty-two. It was freak and gut-wrenching. Losing her, especially like that destroyed him for over eight years. Zax eventually took over for our father as the CEO of Monroe Fashion, our family's luxury fashion label, when our piece of shit father did some unscrupulous things. Last year our ex-stepsister Aurelia became his design intern and after some serious drama, they fell in love. Now it's a lot of smiles and laughs, which seriously make me smile and laugh in return.

He was the grumpiest fucker on the planet before she came into his life.

Suzie was like a big sister to me. We were as close as close could be. Our band Central Square was our love child. It was the dream we both shared, her our manager and me the front man.

"Except we both know there already is one perfect woman out there for you."

And just like that, my world shuts down.

"You could look her up," he continues casually as if he's not scrambling my insides and frying them in searing hot butter like the eggs I'm eating.

"Fuck you." I practically snarl the words at him, my hand fisting around my butter knife. He knows better than to bring her up to me like this. It's one thing when our friend and former bandmate Asher jokes around, but Zax? No. Not cool.

A nonchalant sip of his coffee. "I'm serious. You could."

I glare, and I do it hard, so he knows just what level of a dick he's being—it's a twelve out of ten, in case you are curious. "I can't. You know I can't." I've forced myself not to hundreds of times. There is no win for me if I do. Nothing changes except reopening ancient wounds. No thanks. I'd just as soon dodge those for the rest of my life.

Zax's eyes cast over my shoulder toward the exit of the restaurant in a contemplative wander. But there is no contemplation with this. With her. My best friend or I guess she was. She's an obsession I haven't been able to shake in the sixteen years since I first laid eyes on her.

But the last time I saw her...

"Where is she living now?"

"Fuck. You!" I repeat, not even bothering to temper the

octave of my voice. We're getting looks, I'm positive about it, but right now I don't care. "Stop, Zax. I'm not kidding around with this. Not her, brother."

The one woman I will *never* have as mine and he knows it.

He sighs. Then he stands, wiping his mouth with his napkin before dropping it onto his half-finished plate. "I have to make a call. Then I likely have to go. So..." His eyes up high toward the exit. "Yep. See ya. Call me. I'm here for you and I love you. Remember that."

With a crinkle in my brow and a what-the-fuck expression, my brother waltzes out of the restaurant with a meager pat on my shoulder, leaving me here alone. Only, it takes less than two seconds to realize why he did that.

A woman takes the bench seat diagonal from me at the table beside mine. I stare. My breath gone. My lungs empty. My mind frazzled. My heart a rave...

Then I blow out a breath. Even and slow. Warmth creeps slowly through me like drugs and I smile like the devil I have occasionally been known to be.

I haven't seen her since that night three or so years ago when she came to my concert in Chicago. We spent the night talking because she told me nothing else could happen, and in that talking, the woman whom I considered to be my best friend, the person to whom I told all my darkest secrets, who knew me inside and out, who I was insanely, disruptively, terminally in love with left me a Dear John note.

Except now here she is, back home in Boston sitting across from me in a random café.

Without hesitation, I climb out of my seat, toss some cash on the table, and then drop down onto the bench directly beside her.

She jumps, her head snapping in my direction, caught off guard by some random weirdo creeping in on her personal space until recognition lights her features. Purple eyes—the most insanely beautiful eyes in the world—grow wider than Fenway Park, her pink glossy lips parting on a surprised breath. Her hair, much shorter than the last time I saw it, flows like ribbons of black ink around her shoulders.

"Hi," I say. "This seat taken?"

"Greyson."

"Fallon," I mock her exaggeration of my name, especially when we never use each other's full names. "Shocker of shockers seeing you here. You don't even like breakfast food."

She swallows audibly. "I… I do now."

"Really?"

She lets out a remorseful laugh, her gaze flickering over to me briefly before it playfully bounces around the restaurant. "No. Not really. Eggs are the slimy food of the devil and pancakes make me feel like I'm eating a loaf of bread doused in sugar. The only thing redeeming about breakfast is bacon. And toast. But that has to stay our little secret."

"We're good at that," I chide, nudging her. "Having our little secrets and even some bigger ones. It's been a thousand years, Fall. You good? I'm good," I say to her since that's always been our thing. Whether we're saying goodbye or hello. "You look beautiful."

Her eyes sparkle and a smile curls up the corner of her lips as we fall back into our old routine. "I'm good. How are you, Grey? Handsome as ever I see."

I wink at her and take her hand from her lap, trying not to think about how smooth and soft it is, and set it down on the seat between us. Then I loop our pinkies together.

"When did you get into town?"

That question does something unexpected to her and suddenly she's staring at me so intently I can see all the flecks of purple and lavender and even touches of blue in her eyes. It pains me that I've gone so long without looking directly into them. I squeeze her finger, but I can feel her resistance, her need to pull away.

She blinks and then blinks again. And in those blinks, I catch her oh shit moment and it hurts. It hurts a lot.

"I... um." She licks her lips, her head bowing slightly, her voice strained with genuine regret. "I've been here, Grey."

"Here?"

She sags further while breathing out the word "Boston."

"For how long, Fall Girl?"

Her pinky clings to mine as her gaze plummets to the empty place setting before her. "Since I finished med school."

Sucker. Punch. Everything inside me freezes over. Like holding an ice cube in your fist, it hurts and it's brutally cold all the while numbing you from within. "Wow."

"I know."

"Do you, babe? You told me you were doing your residency in Miami. You lied to me."

"Yes. I lied," she admits, shame consuming her features even as she leans ever so slightly against me, shoulder to shoulder now. "I did my residency at Boston Children's Hospital and at Hughes Healthcare."

"Jesus." I run my free hand across my face. "I don't even know what to say to that. All this time? Why? Why didn't you tell me?"

Vulnerability and dismay drip from her voice as she says, "I'm sorry. I hated myself for the lie and I hated myself for being back in Boston and not telling you, especially anytime I knew you were here." Her gaze climbs back up to mine. "It hurt like hell. Not seeing you, not telling you, keeping something like that from you. I didn't have a choice though, Grey. I didn't."

"You could have told me the truth."

"No. I couldn't have," she says adamantly, but her fierceness crumbles before me. Suddenly she looks wrecked, exhausted, her weight falling heavily against me, her head on my shoulder, and fuck it if anyone is taking pictures or not. She squeezes my pinky again and tilts her head, staring ruefully up at me. "If you knew I was here, we would have seen each other, and I couldn't see you. It was difficult enough for me to hold back." A hard swallow and then her gaze lands on our joined pinkies. "I told you the last time I saw you..."

"No, you left me a note that never told me why," I accuse. "I woke up in that hotel room and found the couch you were supposed to be sleeping on empty. A fucking note on hotel stationary saying goodbye."

A note I've since burned because reading it over and over again was nothing short of self-destructive. Not that I needed the actual note. I had memorized it. Examined every dark scrawl of her inked words.

I ran after her. She doesn't even know it. I hopped on that flight to Miami, and she wasn't even ever in Miami. Fuck. Just fuck!

"I'm engaged," she blurts out, righting her body. I stare at her, positive I did not just hear those words from her sweet lips. "Engaged? Since when?"

"Two weeks. The notice is going out publicly this week. We waited for political reasons since the mid-term elections are coming up and both of our fathers are running for senatorial reelection." She emits a mournful sigh. "I should have told you. I know this. I've thought about it so many times, but I..."

She trails off just as the door of the restaurant swings open, and in walks a dude who screams aristocrat. His blue eyes sparkle, his short blond hair is expensively cut and perfectly coiffed, and his Monroe suit—which inherently makes me want to kill him since it's my family's brand—is expertly tailored. He does a sweep of the restaurant, not immediately finding Fallon, but I know that's who he's searching for.

I know it the same way I know how to play any song I hear once without sheet music.

"To him?" I point incredulously. Fallon's other hand covers mine, lowering it back to my lap and I take her hand, holding it firmly, touching the ring on her finger. My stomach sinks like lead. It's a big diamond, I'll give the prick that much.

"Yes. Grey… I…"

Finally, he locates Fallon and the smile that erupts across his face has my jaw clenching. Why didn't Zax drag me out of here when he saw her enter? Why didn't he save me from this? I should—could—get up and walk away. Walk right out of the damn restaurant, but I can't seem to make my legs move. *Engaged?* How in the fuck did that happen?

She's going to marry this guy? *Marry him*? No. She can't.

"Bacchus," she murmurs, her hands releasing both of mine as she slips around the other side of the table and stands.

I choke on a laugh. *Bacchus?!* For real?

"Dumpling!"

"Dumpling?" I repeat and she kicks my shin under the table before she rounds it and greets him with a kiss on the cheek—not the lips, I note—and then sits back down beside me.

"And who is this?" he asks, taking the chair opposite us and setting his napkin down on his lap. Eyeing me with a look I'm all too familiar with. One that says he knows exactly who I am, and he doesn't like it one bit.

"Greyson, this is my fiancé, Bacchus Hastings Astley the fourth. Bacchus, this is Greyson Monroe—"

"The original," I cut her off. Fallon coughs out a laugh but quickly stifles it. Bacchus Astley. Son of a senator. Naturally. I stretch out my hand and he grips it, but it's limp compared to the death grip I'm giving him. I smile. It isn't friendly. He returns it, and for a few moments, we do the male sizing-each-other-up thing.

He releases my hand first and I win, though there is no victory to be had for me.

"It's nice to meet you, Greyson. Fallon never mentioned you

before. How long have you two known each other since I assume you didn't just meet now?"

"Funny, she never mentioned you to me either."

He makes a displeased noise in the back of his throat and Fallon pinches my thigh.

I redirect. "I imagine she wouldn't have told you about me. Her family doesn't like me too much. Fallon and I used to be neighbors growing up. I was friends with her brother Dillon before the accident."

Fallon shifts beside me, her foot rubbing mine. She hates it when I blame myself for the accident with Dillon. I want to throw my arm around her shoulder or retake her hand, but I restrain myself. Just barely.

"How long have you two been together?" I toss back at him, though I'm pretty positive I already know the answer. I never looked her up. I never had the stomach for it, but now I feel foolish for that.

"Three years," he tells me arrogantly, and yep, it's all coming together now.

"Interesting. That's exactly how long it's been since I saw her last."

Another pinch, this one harder, and yeah, I likely shouldn't have said that. Or still, be here since her family can't know we kept in touch after I left when we were teenagers.

"Hmmm," he says, appraising me with a tilt of his head and narrowing of his eyes. After a beat, a smug smile twists his lips, and he snaps his fingers in that "aha" way as if he's just figured out who I am and didn't already know. Douche. "You're one of those boy banders, right? From that band that broke up all those years ago after that girl died." Fallon stiffens beside me at the mention of Suzie's death, but her dirtbag fiancé doesn't catch it before he continues with, "What was it called again... Harvard Square?"

"Central Square," she corrects for me.

His gaze snaps sharply over to hers. “You’re a fan?”

“You know I am, Bacchus. I have his concert T-shirt in my closet and his music on my phone. You’ve caught me listening to it several times.”

That shouldn’t give me as much satisfaction as it does.

“Well, now I know why.”

“It’s good music,” I cut in to take the heat off her. “You should give it a listen too. Though technically we were never considered a boy band. Now I play as a solo artist. What do you do?”

He squares his shoulders and sets his folded hands on the edge of the table. “I’m a partner in a law firm, but one day I hope to follow in my father’s footsteps and run for office.”

I grin. “Of course you do. The Larks wouldn’t have set their daughter up with anyone else.”

“How did you know they set us up?”

“Greyson,” Fallon hisses under her breath, and I need to stop this before it ends badly for her.

“Lucky guess, but what a small world that I ran into Fallon here.” I turn and take her in, wanting to continue to be angry and hostile, but it’s impossible. I know Fallon. A hell of a lot better than this douchebag does or ever will. I know why she didn’t tell me she was doing her residency here and I know why she’s engaged to this guy.

I want to ask her if she actually loves him. If he’s the guy for her and if she’s happy. If she’s happy, well, at least then this would be easier to swallow. I always swore I wouldn’t be another person in her life to demand things of her. Especially things I know she can’t give me.

Like herself. Like her time. Like her heart.

Now… now she’s going to marry him and there is nothing I can do to stop it. No matter how much the thought feels like someone is stabbing me with a jagged knife and twisting it around in my chest. I have to protect myself. Unwittingly she tried and now I'm looking at this guy and I'm an open, bleeding mess of a man.

Not something I manage well, so I do what I do best and shut it down. Only this time, it's not working. This feeling. It's refusing to be brushed off or locked away. It's a twenty-ton boulder on my chest, restricting my breathing and making everything hurt like a son of a bitch.

I clear my throat. "Well, I'll let you two enjoy your breakfast." I stand and her eyes follow me, saying so many things to me. Things like I'm sorry and this hurts and I miss you and I wish, I wish, I wish. "Take care of yourself, Fall." I turn to her fiancé who is watching us carefully. "Nice meeting you, man."

I smack his shoulder and head for the exit, my heart in my feet making my steps heavy. I stop short, blinking at the rays of sunshine as they shine through the glass door, thinking. Before I can talk myself out of it, I slip my small notebook and pen I occasionally use to write song lyrics from my back pocket and scribble down a quick message. Then I tear the sheet from the spirals and fold it in quarters and tuck it into my palm.

I'll never get another chance again. Might as well take it. She left me a note and now I'm returning the favor. Though mine is very different from hers.

Turning back around, I realize she's still watching me even as she's speaking to him. I smile because damn, she takes my breath away, and then I return to her table. "How rude of me. I forgot to congratulate you on your engagement. I hope you're as happy as you look."

I lean in and press my lips to her cheek while at the same time, I clasp her hand and slip her the folded piece of paper. She takes it, her brows pinched questioningly even as her breath catches. Her hand closes around the paper and I release her.

Walking away.

This time I don't look back. My message was delivered. It's

hers now and I feel better for her having it. Knowing I'll never see her again after today.

Want to know what happens next with Grey and Fallon? Keep reading Irresistibly Perfect today and get lost in this best friends to lovers, second chance, forced proximity, brother's best friend romance today!

Milton Keynes UK
Ingram Content Group UK Ltd.
UKHW040640040923
428018UK00001B/104